SULLIVAN: COWBOY PROTECTOR

THE KAVANAGH BROTHERS BOOK 4

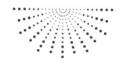

KATHLEEN BALL

Dedication

This book is dedicated to all of you who have helped me get it published-Thank You!!!
And as always to Bruce, Steven, Colt, Clara and Mavis because I love them.

CHAPTER ONE

Sheila Kelly leaned over, bracing her hand against the rough tree trunk. Her lungs burned and her legs felt like rubber. Her breaths came in loud gasps, and it was hard to hear if she was still being pursued. She'd dealt with all kinds, but she'd never been chased by men with rifles.

"Witch!" someone shouted.

Pushing away from the tree, she took off running again. Why couldn't they understand? There hadn't been a way to save the little girl; she'd been dead before they brought her into Sheila's cabin. But they'd put the blame on Sheila and gotten themselves worked up. When they had mentioned burning her at the stake, she took off running out the back door.

Her face, hands and arms were covered in scratches from the limbs of the trees and bushes. A few of the cuts were deep, but that didn't matter. She had to get away, but where was she supposed to go? Those men would get the whole town roused against her, and they'd surely hang her. She had to get her daughter and then find a way to leave the area completely.

"Oof!" She hit the ground hard as she tripped over a root. Wetness trickled into her mouth and she touched it with her fingertips. They came back coated with red liquid. Ugh. Her nose was bleeding. And her ankle throbbed. Still, she needed to get away. *Think, think, what to do?* Would they expect her to run to town to get help? Then she would go the other way. She turned north and ran until she came to a fence.

Going any farther was impossible; her ankle needed to rest. She slumped against a big oak tree near the fence and slid down until she lay on the ground, hoping the underbrush would hide her.

Closing her eyes, she prayed for protection. She was a healer, not a witch. She'd healed so many of the people who lived in the area, but today all good deeds went out the window and blew away in a fierce wind to be forgotten because she couldn't bring a dead child back to life. She was mostly forgotten as it was… unless someone couldn't get to the doctor or the doctor was away. Otherwise she lived a hermit type of life and had since she was thirteen.

Breathing became easier and her nose stopped bleeding. When it was safe, she'd make herself a crutch from branches and go where no one could find her. Waiting until dark would be for the best. Now if only she could get her heart to stop hammering.

The pounding of hooves alerted her. They sounded to be coming from all sides. This was it. She trembled. What would it feel like to hang?

One horse and rider were on the other side of the fence while the other was almost stepping on her. The quaking of her body wouldn't stop.

"Howdy, Russ," a familiar voice greeted.

"Kavanagh. I'm looking for that healing woman. She killed little Jenny Wren. I need to talk to her."

"Saw her last week. She was home with her daughter. Haven't seen her since then, though."

"Thanks, Kavanagh, I'll keep looking," Russ said, sounding determined.

As soon as the sound of hoofbeats diminished into the distance, she opened her eyes and released her breath.

Sullivan vaulted the fence. "It's just me," he said in a low voice.

"I need your help, Sullivan," she pleaded. "Becca is at Widow Muse's place and I need to get her before they take her away." Tears escaped her eyes and trailed down her face.

Sullivan kneeled before her. His blue eyes were full of purpose as he touched a few of her scratches. Their eyes met, and she felt less shaky.

"I can't walk, I hurt my ankle. I could walk with a crutch. But I'd rather stay here if you'd get Becca for me."

"I'd feel better getting you home first." His strong jaw set.

"No, get Becca... please?"

He reached forward and wiped a tear off her face with his thumb. Then he stood and looked around and picked up a branch that he handed Sheila. "See if you can use this."

She nodded. It would serve as a good crutch.

"Donnell and Murphy are supposed to be checking the pasture for any poisonous plants the cattle can get into. Wave them down if you see them and have them bring you to the house."

"Thank you, Sullivan—" But he'd already jumped the fence, hopped on his bay, and was riding away.

DIDN'T people understand Sheila didn't have a mean bone in her body? He hoped he didn't meet any armed yahoos out in the forest. Russ' friends were the shoot first ask questions later type. He rode slowly and silently and made it to the widow's house without a problem. He tied Zealous at the back of the house.

The rear door opened, and a white-haired woman appeared. "Quick, take her to safety. Those men were already here, and I put them off, but I bet they'll be back. Bless you, Sullivan." She shoved a dark-haired little girl into his arms.

"You be careful," he told the widow as he mounted the horse with Becca in his arms.

"Don't you worry none about me," she assured him.

He tipped his hat and slowly rode away.

Becca kept turning, trying to see his face, and he leaned down to her ear. "We need to be so very quiet. I'm taking you to your ma."

Her head dropped forward and he hugged her to him for a moment. She was such a quiet child to begin with. There were kids on the Kavanagh ranch she could play with at least.

Sullivan was confident his nine brothers would help him keep Sheila and Becca safe. His gut tightened thinking about Sheila and her daughter being in danger. He urged Zealous to go faster. It didn't take long before he was in front of the ranch house. He swung down with Becca in his arms.

"You'd best get her inside," Donnell advised. "Sheila is all kinds of worried."

Good, so his brothers had found her, then. He nodded his thanks and practically raced up the steps of the big house. Once in the door, Becca squirmed until she was standing on the wood planked floor. She flew into her mother's arms and cried.

"Are you hurt? Let me look at you." Sheila peeled Becca's tightly wound arms from her neck. "Did anyone touch you?"

Becca shook her head. "Just Sullivan. I like him, but I was scared." She dove against Sheila's body again and buried her face.

Sheila met his gaze and mouthed, *"Thank you."*

The fear in her eyes got to him. Sheila was as fearless as they came. It couldn't be easy raising a child alone, though Sheila made it look like it was.

His relief at Sheila's safety engulfed him, overwhelmed him, making him feel uneasy. He liked to care, but this was bordering on caring too much.

Dolly bustled out of the kitchen with a small tray. She set a cup of tea and a glass of milk on the table. When she peered up at Sullivan, he nodded his gratitude. Dolly had been taking care of the family for as long as he could remember. With their parents gone, she had taken on the role of mother and friend. Sighing, she went back into the kitchen, returning in a few moments with a plate of cookies and a cup of tea of her own.

"It sounds like you both had an awful fright." She put the cookies on the table in front of mother and daughter, and then she sat on one of the chairs near the sofa. "Did you manage to bring any of your things with you?"

"It all happened too fast. It was all I could do to escape. Jenny Wren's father carried her into the house. She was already dead. But he didn't want to believe me. The next thing I knew he started to yell it was my fault the girl had died. Russ and a few of his friends were outside, and that's when I heard them talking about burning the witch. I saw them head for my front door and I ran out the back and down a hidden path."

"You poor dear." Dolly commiserated.

Teagan, the oldest of the brothers, burst into the house and Gemma his wife hurried down the stairs. Sullivan cringed. Gemma shouldn't have gone down the steps so quickly. She was heavy with child and out of breath. Teagan seated her.

"Oh, your ankle is black and blue!" Gemma exclaimed, pointing at Sheila's foot.

Dolly immediately stood. "I'll get a cold wet cloth to wrap it. Donnell pull that chair closer so I can put her leg up on it."

Dolly came back with the cloth and wrapped Sheila's ankle.

"That feels better. Thank you."

"What else do you need? You probably know a plant to cure it."

"Actually, Sullivan if you have the liniment, I gave you for the horses, that would be wonderful." She glanced at Dolly and then at Gemma. "I have cuts on my shoulder that need stitches. Are either of you...?"

"Your best bet is to have Sullivan do it. He has a way of stitching that makes a scar less noticeable."

Gemma nodded in agreement. "Dolly and I are constantly using a needle but when it comes to stitches in skin, Sullivan is the one you want."

"Sullivan, carry her to the front bedroom." Dolly instructed. "It has a big bed Sheila and Becca can share."

"I'll get the water heated and gather the soap, cloths, thread and needle," Gemma volunteered as she struggled to get up from the plush chair. She laughed as she gave up and held out her hands for Teagan to take.

"Gemma, I'll do all that," Dolly instructed. "Donnell, could you go over to Quinn's place and see if Heaven can bring the kids over to keep Becca company?" She turned and stared at Sullivan. "Well? What are you waiting for? Donnell grab the liniment while you're out."

Teagan and Gemma exchanged amused glances.

"Teagan, you hurry on ahead of Sullivan and make sure the bed covers are turned down."

Sullivan's lips twitched. Dolly was good in a crisis, but he'd never noticed before how bossy she was.

"Ready?" He gazed into Sheila's dark eyes. When she nodded, he lifted her into his arms. "You can help too, Becca."

Sheila wrapped her arms around his neck, and he felt her breath. It warmed his whole insides. He made his strides a bit longer; he needed to put her down. He was not in the market for a female, especially a carefree one who thumbed her nose at all of society's rules. She was very attractive, and he enjoyed talking with her, but that was where it stopped.

Teagan turned down the bed, and Sullivan gently set Sheila on it.

Why was he the one who had to stitch her up? Gemma, Ciara, and Heaven all sewed. It was going to be very awkward touching her skin. Hopefully, it was just her arm or something.

Soon enough, everything was brought into the room and everyone was ushered out except for him. This couldn't be proper, but Sheila didn't seem bothered by it.

"I could ask one of the women to stay in here," he offered.

"We're adults, Sullivan. Open the door if you're concerned."

He did just that, but he still didn't feel right.

CHAPTER TWO

They'd become good friends in the last few years, and now Sullivan acted as though she was contagious. Had she done or said something wrong? His was the one friendship she'd treasured. He wanted nothing from her. He differed from the men in town. Most of them assumed her to be a lonely, desperate woman.

"I'll need to take my dress off, but I have proper undergarments and of course we'll use the sheet to cover me." Usually she said those words to patients to make them comfortable. How odd to be on the other side of things. She unbuttoned her dress and slid it off, hissing at the searing pain. "Worse than I thought. I can do it myself, Sullivan." She glanced at him over her shoulder.

He turned and his eyes went wide when he looked at her shoulders and back. "What happened?"

"Running through the woods and falling." She fisted her hands.

"Painful?"

"Yes, and I don't have my willow bark tea." She drew a fortifying breath and tried to slacken her muscles, knowing it would go easier if she wasn't tense. "It's fine, just get started. Clean the wound before you stitch."

"I have some whiskey," he offered. "I bet it would help with the pain, too."

A shudder rippled through her. "No, thank you. I don't drink whiskey."

He carefully cleaned two spots on her left side. "I will have to sit on the bed to reach the first one."

"That's fine." She needed him to just do it and get the whole thing over with.

The mattress dipped when he sat. She gritted her teeth as the needle went in. Deep breathing helped to manage the pain a bit.

At the sound of approaching footsteps, she turned her head, surprised when Teagan entered the room. "Gemma sent this up for you to drink." He handed her a teacup.

She smelled it and smiled. "Willow bark. Tell Gemma I thank her." She drank it and waited for its effect. Her body began to relax slightly.

"Do you need me, Sullivan?" Teagan asked.

"I'm almost done. Make sure you leave the door open," he quipped.

Teagan chuckled. "I'm not worried. You've always been the protector, not the one who causes trouble."

Sheila turned to give Sullivan easier access to the other side of her back. She tried not to flinch at even his softest of touches, but she couldn't help it. Despite the willow bark tea, she felt the pricks of the needle and the pulling of the thread. Her mind kept repeating what had happened. Surely, people didn't believe in witches anymore, did they? That Mr. Wren had certainly gotten people believing enough to search for her, though.

She needed her rainy-day money, and she needed to take her daughter and run. She'd been wise enough to have bags packed and money hidden, but she hadn't planned where to go. Texas was a big state, but much of it was unsettled. They weren't awfully far from Oklahoma. She could go there... find a job that didn't involve her vast knowledge of healing.

"What do you know about Oklahoma?" she asked, trying to keep her voice nice and light.

"Not all that much." He pulled another stitch through. "It's not a territory yet, and there are plenty of Indians, Choctaw Indians. It's settled some, but you can't expect any help if the Indians decide they want you off their land."

"That bad, huh? My family has lived in this area for generations. They must have had to fight to keep their land at some point. I think I'm the first to be run off." Frustration had a hold on her.

"You planning on taking a trip?" She couldn't see his face, but she could tell from his voice he didn't approve. She'd never needed any man's approval before and never intended to.

"I need to take Becca to a safe place. I'm not sure which way I plan to go. I also need to stop by my place and grab a few things and then dig up my money."

"You might want to wait a few days. Your house is certain to be watched."

Frantic pounding on the front door caused her to jump.

Sullivan cursed under his breath and held her in place while he tied off the thread and set the needle down.

"I don't want anyone here to be hurt," she blurted, ignoring the sting in her back from where the thread had pulled when she'd moved. "I'll just give myself up, unless there's another way out of here. But Becca... she needs to be kept safe. Most folks don't know I have a child."

"Stay put." He stood and stepped in front of her, staring hard. "I mean it."

11

She gave him a curt nod. But he'd soon learn he couldn't boss her around.

———

SULLIVAN JOINED the rest downstairs and nodded to the man that he'd come across that morning. "What's going on?" Sullivan asked Teagan.

"Russ here says Sheila Kelly killed a girl, but he doesn't know how she did it. Something smells fishy about the whole story."

Sullivan turned to Russ. "How was she killed? Did Sheila shoot her?"

"No, nothing like that. Ed brought his daughter into the Kelly place and the next thing we knew, Jenny was dead."

"But how sick was she, and why did Ed bring her there?" Sullivan gazed intently at Russ.

"The way I heard it; Jenny caught her dress on fire while watching her ma wash clothes. They soaked her in cold water for a long time. Then one of the men was called to hitch up the wagon. They made a pallet in back for Jenny and we hurried to town, leaving the missus behind. That pretty nurse said the doctor wasn't in. She told Ed to take Jenny to Sheila." Russ shrugged. "We all rode to the witch's house."

"Have you ever seen a burned person, Russ?" Teagan asked. "Cold water helps a bit, but the burned flesh is an awful sight. She would have been in too much pain for them to put clothes on her. Did you hear any crying?" He took on a thoughtful expression. "Unless maybe Jenny was given medicine when it happened. Give too much and it can kill a person."

"She was limp and dressed with her eyes closed. That's all I saw. Never heard no crying." A frown creased his forehead. "You made some good points, but I doubt you'd be able to change Mr. Wren's mind. He told me once that Sheila had put a curse on him, and he believed it." Sighing, he shook his head. "I'll go back and try to reason with them, but I know my voice won't be heard above the rest of the men who are out for blood."

Becca walked to Sullivan and held her arms up to him. He immediately picked her up and snuggled her close.

Russ stared at him hard. "I never knew you had a child."

Sullivan smiled. "She's my pride and joy." He wasn't about to mention her name.

Teagan walked Russ to the door and practically pushed him out.

"He won't be the last to come here," Gemma said in a low voice. "That poor girl must have been dead before they dressed her."

"I'm going to carry Becca upstairs. Dolly could you please make up a tray for her and her mama? I think we must move them tomorrow."

The door opened and Brogan stepped inside, quickly closing the door behind him. He wore an expression of surprise. "I just got a visit," he said right off. "I have a feeling they won't stop until they find Sheila."

"Good to see you, Brogan," Dolly said as she started to climb the steps with a platter of food. Sullivan walked behind her tenderly carrying the little girl.

"Teagan, we'd better list possibilities of hideouts," Brogan said.

Sullivan gave Becca a sad smile. He should have protected them somehow. He should have seen this coming. There must have been *something* he could have done. As soon as they walked into the bedroom, Becca squirmed down and ran to her mother.

The affection between the two always marveled Sullivan. It was a sight to behold. Sheila winced as she moved to hug

13

Becca, so Sullivan lifted the little girl and sat her on the bed right next to her mother.

"There, this way you can both eat supper in bed."

Sheila mouthed *"thank you"* to him.

"If you need anything just holler," Dolly told her as she bustled out the room.

Sullivan put the tray on Sheila's lap and then sat on the bed, helping Becca. She was a good eater and polite too.

"We'll have to move you and Becca tomorrow," he casually told Sheila.

Her eyes filled with fear. "What do you mean? Move us where? I thought it would just blow over and I'd have time to collect my things then move on."

"I don't think it will go that way for now. Don't worry, I'll be with you every step of the way."

"I still need to get my clothes, my medicines, and my money." Her voice grew louder.

"It'll have to wait."

"Take this tray off me. Take it now!"

Obliging her, he lifted the tray, and she scrambled out of bed, wincing as she turned toward him. "I don't like people telling me what to do. I have my own life." She hobbled in front of the bed. "I want to be consulted on decisions. I'm not a mindless person who just follows the dictates of others." She frowned as he spread butter on a piece of bread and handed it to Becca. "If you don't mind, I can help my daughter."

She waited until he left the room and then she shut the door.

Shaking his head at how bristly she'd become, he went downstairs. Donnell greeted him with a grin, his eyes full of humor. "Kicked you out didn't she?"

Sullivan rubbed the back of his neck as he scowled.

"We all know you're sweet on her," Donnell teased.

It would have been so easy to just punch Donnell and get his frustrations out that way. "It doesn't matter. We need to see to her safety." He brushed by Donnell, hitting his brother's shoulder with his own. "She wants to be consulted in any decisions. I'm not sure that's in her best interest." Sullivan shrugged.

Gemma and Dolly both turned on him at the same time, each wearing a shocked expression.

"Sullivan Kavanagh, sit!" Dolly pointed to one of the wooden chairs at the table.

Uh oh. First and last name. He must have done something wrong. He sat and waited.

"Does she have a condition I don't know about? Are her thoughts scrambled?" She put her hands on her hips as she stared at him.

"No, ma'am," he answered in a subdued voice.

His brothers snickered in the background.

"She's been raising that beautiful girl all by herself for some time now, hasn't she?"

He slowly nodded.

"Then what makes you think you can run her life without asking her? You might think of her as a damsel in distress, but she's capable of taking care of herself. Do you think Gemma, Ciara, or Heaven would allow their husbands to tell them what to do?"

Sullivan pushed back his chair, causing a loud scraping noise. "I get the point. I'm not stupid."

Dolly hurried over and hugged him. "No one said you were. It's just that I see how you two eye each other when the other isn't looking. Don't push her away."

He took a deep breath and gritted his teeth. They didn't understand him at all. "Let's get a few ideas so we can ask her what she'd like to do."

The door opened again, and this time the rest of his

brothers all filed in. Murphy, Fitzpatrick, Angus, Rafferty, and finally Shea.

"Horses coming. A lot of them," Murphy announced.

Quinn came in the back door with Heaven, Owen, Tim, along with Daisy, Ciara, and Orla. Orla locked the door behind her.

Brogan put his arm around Ciara and nodded at his sister-in-law, Orla.

"Women and children upstairs and stay down away from the windows," Teagan yelled right before he kissed Gemma.

The brothers all scrambled for extra ammo. Then Quinn put out the lanterns while everyone took their places near the windows.

"Why are they back?" Donnell asked.

"They must know Sheila and Becca are here," Murphy answered.

"Russ saw Becca, and someone probably told him I don't have a daughter," Sullivan said in

frustration.

CHAPTER THREE

"*S*end out the witch!"

Sheila gasped. She sat with Becca and the others on the floor of a back bedroom. Ciara had the door open and she guarded them with a rifle. Heaven stood to the side of the window, doing the same.

Sheila heard yelling back and forth with promises of no one getting hurt if they sent her out. Her gut clenched, and tears filled her eyes. She couldn't put this many people in danger. She kissed the top of Becca's head and slowly stood. Then despite the pain in her ankle, she rushed past Ciara and almost went tumbling down the stairs. Sullivan caught her before she hit the ground.

"What are you doing?" It was too dark to see him, but his voice was full of anger.

"I'm giving myself up. What if someone gets killed because of me?" Her voice quivered.

"I'm trying to defend you, and you are just making it harder!" he hissed.

"Both of you, I need to talk to you in the kitchen, stay down," Teagan said.

Teagan followed them and opened the pantry door. "Sheila, grab a couple of lanterns."

Sheila went in, but it was dark. The next thing she knew Sullivan was pushed into her and she heard the sound of the door locking.

"What is going on?" She cried.

"No noise. Whisper," Teagan said before his footsteps faded away.

"Sullivan?" she whispered; afraid tears would fall.

"He tricked us. I knew the lanterns were on the top shelf and you wouldn't be able to reach them. He didn't want us arguing and giving away our position."

"What if someone dies? I can't live with that." She was pulled roughly into Sullivan's arms, and she grabbed onto the back of his shirt, afraid he'd let go. "What about Becca?"

"My brothers will make sure she is fine."

They were quiet, listening for any hint of what was going on.

"Let's sit," Sullivan suggested. He let go of her and sat on the floor. Then he guided her until she was sitting with her back against his chest. There wasn't much room.

"No one has been accused of being a witch since my great, great, great grandmother," she murmured. "It's always in the back of each Kelly woman's mind. But I never thought — I mean in these modern times who believes in witches? Maybe history is just repeating itself. None of us ever married, but we each had a girl child. I knew it would just be a matter of time before fate turned on me, so I always carried a knife with me." She lifted a shoulder and let it fall. "One day I couldn't get to it, and the result was Becca."

"They have no cause to call you a witch. Teagan will talk them down. Then it'll blow over once Ed Wren thinks about what the truth is." He hesitated, but she sensed he wanted to say something else, so she kept silent. "I am sorry for what happened to you. Not all men are like that." His voice was gentle.

"I do have a few books about spells and curses. My mother left me one about the history of witchcraft. We were looking for a way to break the cycle. We wanted to be mothers but with a man of our own choosing."

"I'm moving us in the morning," he announced abruptly. "There's a cabin not too far from here, but not on our property either. Quinn, Heaven, and the kids stayed there when they were being chased by outlaws. I think it's our best chance until things settle down."

Her heart dropped. He wasn't asking, he was dictating. She sighed. Then again, she wasn't in a position to oppose his plan. This was probably one of the reasons the Kelly women never married. They were too independent.

"We'll be ready, Sullivan," she promised. "You could just leave us there. I know you have a lot of work to do with the cows calving and all."

He wrapped his arms around her. "That's the beauty of having so many brothers, I won't be missed."

"Becca has taken to you."

"I like her. She's sweet." His voice spoke of kindness. "I haven't heard anything from outside in a while. Maybe they'll let us out of here."

"I'm not happy about being tricked into this closet, but truthfully I haven't been held since my ma died. I have Becca, but it's not the same. Drawing comfort from another adult is a real blessing."

He released a soft chuckle. "We're lucky we have Dolly. One look at our faces, and she knows what's going on inside us. Since the war, I've come to cherish her caring nature."

He rubbed his hands up and down her arms. There was something about him that brought butterflies to her stomach. She'd never felt this way and decided to enjoy it while it lasted. She'd never marry. She'd always known that. Though she never questioned her fate, she wondered now... why couldn't a Kelly woman marry? Sullivan was too overbearing for her, and they'd be sure to butt heads. But maybe there was another?

The door opened, and Becca ran in and shut it behind her and then curled up on her mother's lap. No one locked the door behind her.

"Are you all right, my precious girl?"

"Yes, Mama. I was scared, but Gemma held me. I like her. She smells like flowers."

Experiencing a moment of bliss shocked Sheila. This must be what a family felt like. A family with a man in it. The door would open any second and her illusion would be gone. Closing her eyes, she just breathed and felt. Sullivan's muscles were strong as she leaned back against him, and his breath was warm on her head. She felt Becca's softness as she snuggled even closer. Her braids felt as shiny as they looked, and her skin was baby soft.

Sheila sniffed, picked up a sweet scent. "You smell like flowers too, Becca."

"Gemma put one drop on my neck and said that I could have another when I'm much older." Her happiness of being treated as special gladdened Sheila's heart.

The door opened, and Quinn stood there, his eyes full of humor. "Are you ever coming out?"

"Seeing as I'm in the back I'm waiting for the women to move first." Sullivan sounded happy.

"As long as you're all comfy. Shall I have blankets sent in?" Quinn chuckled.

"I don't want to sleep in a closet," Becca whispered.

Quinn reached in and picked Becca up. "You won't have to, but it is getting mighty late. I know a right comfy bed upstairs."

Sheila scrambled to stand. "I'll take her. Can you thank your brothers for me, Quinn? I didn't hear any shooting."

"Teagan went out on the front porch and told them you weren't here... and that they had at least ten rifles trained on them. They left, but they weren't happy. Oh, and Ciara is mad that you pushed her out of the way."

She took Becca into her arms. "Thank you, Quinn."

———

THE NEXT MORNING BEFORE DAWN, Sullivan had the two females dressed as males and on a horse riding toward the cabin. Both Sheila and Becca had worn the same mutinous expressions on their faces when Sullivan handed them the clothes. He hightailed it out of the room before they had a chance to say no.

He did allow time for coffee and a biscuit. Becca had milk. He'd had supplies already delivered by a couple of his brothers in the late hours of the night. He wasn't taking any chances. When he and Rafferty and Shea had sneaked over to her place, they found her house had been burned down; these men meant business. Apprehension coiled in his gut. How was he supposed to tell her about the house? It was bound to break her heart.

Perhaps it would be better to just wait. Nothing could be done, but she'd only fume about it. He drew Zealous to a stop and jumped down off the bay's back. Then he went to help Sheila, but she already was on the ground with Becca safely in her arms. He'd been looking forward to helping her. He scowled. These were not thoughts he should be having.

"Is something wrong?"

He shook his head. "Just thinking is all. This is it. Go on inside." He opened the door and quickly ushered them into the cabin. "I'll put the horses up. Stay in here."

As he made the horses comfortable in the small barn, he sighed. Why didn't she smile at him anymore? He was trying to keep her and Becca alive. She had said she wanted to be involved, but there hadn't been enough time to consult her. She had to know he was doing this for her. He frowned. Same thing every time; his help either wasn't enough or wasn't wanted. How did a person know what was too much? Not enough got your fellow soldiers killed. Maybe she didn't understand how much danger she was in. Had Sheila made arrangements for Becca in case something happened?

He hadn't expected it to be easy, but he'd thought they were friends.

"Did you know there is only one bed?" Sheila asked as soon as he came inside. She had her arms crossed in front of her, and she was wearing what was becoming a perpetual scowl.

"I'm sleeping on the floor. I did know." It was heartening to see the fire crackling in the big stone fireplace, and even more so when he spotted the coffee. He grabbed a kitchen cloth and wrapped it around the coffee pot handle. "Can I pour you a cup?" As soon as the words were out, he suppressed a wince. She probably wanted to do it herself.

"Thank you, that would be nice."

Surprised, he poured coffee into two tin cups. He set the pot back on some cooler coals and put the rag on the mantel. He handed her the cup. "Becca's sleeping?"

"Yes, she's napping. She was up much earlier than usual."

Was that some type of dig at him? "We have enough wood inside to keep the fire going all day and night. I don't want anyone going outside and drawing attention."

She stared at him. "What about the outhouse? Or did *you* decide we won't need it today?"

He opened his mouth and then shut it. "Would you rather I left you here alone?"

"That's not what I said." She crossed her arms in front of her.

There was a rapid knock on the door, and Sullivan opened it right away. Brogan slipped in quickly.

"You'll need to put the fire out. Men are at the ranch nosing around. Do you want me to take the horses? You could always hide in the tunnel."

"What tunnel?"

"When you played here, you probably never found it. See how the fireplace is framed out on each side with large sections of sanded wood?" He went to the section farthest from the door. He tapped the side and it opened. Inside, below the opening, was a sturdy ladder. "The tunnel doesn't go far, but far enough to get you away and able to run for help. You can lock it from the inside if needed."

"Take the horses and we'll hunker down here. Keep me posted."

"Will do. Stay safe." Brogan slowly opened the door, peered around and then closed it behind him.

CHAPTER FOUR

"*H*ow could you have done that?"

"Done what?"

Sheila took a step toward him. "Let him take our only real way to escape. I'm wondering if I shouldn't just take Becca and leave. I don't think this will work out. I know you're putting your neck out for me, but your decisions make me nervous. Maybe we should take our chances and go home."

His face was full of dread and compassion.

"What? Something has happened. Tell me," she insisted.

He took another step until he was right in front of her. He put his warm hands on her shoulders. "There's no easy way to tell you. Your house and barn were burned down last night. From what I heard, there isn't anything left."

Her stomach churned. The enormity of her loss encompassed her, and her legs began to shake. Everything was gone. How was that possible? She wanted to cry out, she needed to cry out, but Becca was sleeping. She placed both hands over her mouth to keep her sobs in as she wept. Sullivan pulled her to him, and she cried against his chest.

She'd been so annoyed at him, and he'd been doing everything to help them. Maybe she was just an awful person.

She was able to cry because of his strength. She'd had to be the strong one for a long time and her emotions felt like a disastrous storm. Sullivan held her and murmured soft words to her like the friend she knew him to be. It wasn't easy for her to lean on someone else. But she was blessed to have Sullivan.

He sat her down on one of the four wooden chairs in the cabin. It felt cold and lonely without him so close.

Sheila swallowed hard. "If I had done things the way I wanted Becca and I would probably be dead. I've always followed my intuition, but now I don't know what to do anymore. When it's safe, I'll dig up my money and go north to a different state. I can find a job. If I change my name and stop being a healer, they won't find me."

"Whoa, there. You're thinking too far into the future, and there is nothing but what ifs in your thinking. I believe in looking ahead, but we need to survive where we are first. You never know, maybe the men who burned your house will go to prison. You have friends you can rely on."

She shook her head as tears still poured down her face. "I don't have friends except for you and Widow Muse. I heal when I'm called, but other than that most folks don't feel comfortable around a woman who has had a child without the benefit of marriage. I never knew why I couldn't go to school with the other kids. Figured our family must have done something horrific at some point. I didn't realize my mother suffered too. She suffered even more when I came home barely able to stand after that man... I didn't understand at the time why she'd bemoaned my fate."

"I'm sorry."

"You have been good to me, and I've tried to fight you the

whole way." She gave a sad shake of her head. "I'm the one who is sorry. I just think about myself."

He gave her the merest of smiles. "You always think about Becca."

"So, what shall we eat that we don't have to cook?"

His Adam's apple bobbed up and down as he swallowed. "I have canned beans."

"Canned beans it is. We'd best set everything out so we know where it is. It'll be dark in here come nightfall. What about rifles? Did you bring one for me?"

"There's two." He stood and checked the shutters. "It's a sturdy place." Next, he got out the beans, three tin plates, and forks, and he put a bucket of water on the table. He unrolled his bedroll and set both rifles on the mantel. "I know it's not the best situation, but we'll need to use the pail in the corner instead of the outhouse."

"It'll be fine. I'm thankful we have a safe place to stay." She gave him a watery smile. "I'm usually not much of a crier. I… well, it doesn't matter. I'll get our night clothes out and put them at the bottom of the bed. What else do we need?"

Sullivan grabbed down three tin cups from a makeshift cupboard.

"I don't understand," she mused out loud. "If the child was dead before she was brought to me, then why blame me? I tended to Jenny many times. She was a clumsy child and she always seemed to have a broken bone. They never went to the doctor, though, not even when that young Dr. Bright set up practice."

"That is odd." Sullivan frowned. "Maybe he needed someone to blame and it was you. Seeing a person burn is unspeakable. I'm not saying it was right, you understand. I'm just thinking out loud."

"Nothing justifies burning down my house!" She stood and limped to one of the windows, hoping to see outside, but the place was built to withstand any attack and there wasn't a crack in the shutters to spy out of.

Sheila was not one to sit and relax. There was always something that needed doing.

"Did you bring along your needlepoint to work on?" He sounded hopeful. He probably couldn't stand her restlessness.

"I don't do needlepoint. And even if I did, I was too busy running for my life to do it. Don't get me wrong, I make nice clothes, but I don't have time to make fancy needlepoint pictures to put up on the wall." She stopped and shook her head. "Not one sister in that big family of yours. You have peculiar notions of what women do. I grow many plants and herbs and what I don't grow I forage for in the woods. I like to have some medicines already mixed. I also try to teach Becca about plants. She's starting to recognize a few. I grow what we need to eat, and I have traps set. I hunt when I can. Chopping wood takes a lot of time too. Then there is the cooking, and clothes need washing. I mostly get paid in meat or some type of food."

"So, the needlepoint idea is out?" He grinned at her, and for a moment she thought her heart would stop. He was such a handsome man. "I threw a few books into my things. Maybe we can read them later."

It was on the tip of her tongue to ask if he could read in the dark, but she didn't want his grin to go away.

"Mama, I'm hungry."

And just like that, the spell was broken... even if it had been a one-sided spell.

ALL HE HEARD all night was tossing and turning. She wasn't sleeping one wink, and neither was he. The bed creaked again, and he'd had enough. Throwing off his blanket, he got up, lit a nub of candle, and went to the bed. Her eyes widened in panic.

"I won't hurt you. I just thought since we both can't sleep, maybe we could talk. It might help you fall asleep."

She hesitated, then she nodded and slipped out of bed. She took an extra blanket to wrap around her.

Sullivan set the candle on the hearth. It flickered dimly, and probably wouldn't be enough light to draw attention seeing as they'd kept the shutters closed.

"It's strange to sit in front of the fireplace when there isn't a fire," he observed.

"I was afraid I'd wake Becca with my constant move-ment. I can't get the thought of everything burning in a fire. Most can't be replaced. My recipe book for medicine was my great grandmother's, and we each added to it along the years. My mother's things are gone. I remember how she saved and saved for one of those big copper tubs. Her smile when she bathed in it was one of bliss, and I had never seen it before. I saved all of Becca's baby clothes, some had been mine..." She put her elbows on her knees and dropped her head into her hands. "Truthfully, there isn't much money buried. We've had a few lean years, but we always get through without complaint. We give our thanks and praise to God."

"I don't believe in God anymore," Sullivan said quietly. "A person can only rely on themselves and what makes sense. I saw so many young boys die because they thought they knew better. I was the captain in charge, and I'd tell them the plan. I would even draw it in the dirt with a stick for better under-standing, and I can't even count how many young men thought they knew better than me and ended up... I'm sorry I'm not painting a very pretty picture. I used to pray... It never helped."

"You're still alive." Her eyes bore into his until he glanced away.

"That's part of the problem; I never asked to be saved." He swallowed hard. He'd never talked about the war to anyone before, and now here he was spilling his guts. She was too delicate to hear his words.

"I kept hoping there wouldn't be a war. Luckily my house was tucked into the forest. I was never bothered. I made a holster for myself and kept it on a belt around my waist. I carried it everywhere. Sometimes I still feel as though I'm not completely outfitted without it."

"It's good to hear you didn't suffer at the hands of the soldiers. How come you never came to school? I saw you once in the general store, and then I'd only catch a glimpse of you now and then." He'd looked for her everywhere he went.

She straightened up and stared into the empty fireplace. "Someone asked if I could turn a boy into a frog. I told my Ma, and I was never allowed to go back…" Sadness tinged her voice as it dropped off.

"I'm sorry to hear that. I just wondered is all. If we weren't at school, we worked the ranch. I never wanted to do anything else. It's in my blood." He turned his body facing her and took one of her cold hands in his. "Is healing what you wanted to do?" Reaching out, he drew the other hand into his as well. "You're so cold."

"The shock of it all, I suppose." She looked as though she was trying to smile, but it didn't happen. "I was never told I could be anything else. My fate was sealed when Becca was conceived. No man would have wanted me heavy with child. By the time of Becca's birth, my name was so muddied, I kept to myself. It was always better that way. I'm good enough to save their kin from death, but not good enough to be acknowledged in a kind way. It's the way of things. It has been for generations."

He gave her hands a light squeeze and let them go. "I'm sorry. I'd have thought people would be grateful to you."

"It's good you came back unhurt. From the war. I bet your family was happy to see you."

He smiled. "They asked if I had any wounds, and when I said no they tried to wrestle me. Dolly took after them, but when the next brother came home, we all did the same thing to welcome him back. I don't have any wounds you can see, but I'm not the same carefree man I was before I left. I knew how to ride and shoot well, and I was moved up in the ranks until whatever I did got men killed. Sometimes it felt like a noose around my neck getting tighter." He needed to lighten the conversation. "I'm here, and that's what matters."

"Yes, it is." She sighed. "Sullivan, how am I going to heal others without the plants and roots I need? What about my livestock? Did they make it out of the barn? Is my garden demolished? Part of me wants to run as far as I can, and another part wants to stay and fight."

He plucked her from her seat and set her on his lap, putting his arms around her. "We'll get it all figured out. Don't worry, I won't allow you to be left with nothing." She smelled of lavender, and he wanted to run his hands through her dark curls, but he set her back on her feet instead. "Let's give sleep another try." His heart was warmed by a real smile spreading across her face. She was feisty as all get out, but she was also vulnerable. It had taken all of his control not to kiss her. She wouldn't welcome it now... or maybe ever. Some women when treated so cruelly didn't want a man to touch them.

CHAPTER FIVE

They had been inside the cabin for a week, and it hadn't been as bad as she'd imagined. Sullivan was a very polite and generous man. She was delighted and grateful for his friendship. He'd read books out loud to entertain them. They'd decided that making a fire would be fine. Actually, Sullivan decided, and it chaffed a bit. She was so used to every decision being hers and it was hard to be told no.

Becca liked him. He'd sat on the floor with her and played. There wasn't anywhere to go, but she was always at his side. Sheila waited for him to get impatient, but so far... he hadn't. She'd often exchanged amused glances with him because of Becca's antics. It was a treasure to share such moments with another. It'd filled part of the void in her heart.

"Mama, I'll have a cookie, please." Her voice was on the demanding side.

"No, Becca. Maybe after supper." What had gotten into her child?

"Sully said I could have a cookie! I want a cookie!" Becca was one hair away from a full-out tantrum.

"Sullivan, was the cookie your idea?" She folded her arms as she subjected him to an accusing glare.

"What's the harm? It's just a cookie."

She took back every kind thought she'd ever had about him.

"Fine, both of you have as many cookies as you like." She opened the door and left. How dare he? Just who did he think he was? Becca was her child, hers! A sob bubbled up and she walked away so she wouldn't be heard. Her shoulders shook as she cried. This was no way to live. She'd done nothing wrong. Why should she have to hide? What gave them the right to burn her out? Why her?

Oh Lord, what have I done? Have I displeased You so? I know getting pregnant without being married is my sin to bear, just as I was my mother's sin. Why? Can I not change things?

Dusk fell upon her rather fast, and she reluctantly went back into the house. As soon as she stepped over the threshold, Becca ran up and hugged her.

"I sorry."

Sheila fell to her knees and grabbed up her girl. "I'm sorry too. I shouldn't have gotten mad and left."

"It scared me, but Sully said you would be back as soon as you were happy again."

Sheila didn't feel generous enough to smile at Sullivan.

"We ate supper, but we waited until you were here before we had one cookie each," Sullivan said softly as he stared into her eyes. His kind eyes made her uncomfortable; they made her feel at fault.

Standing, she lifted Becca into her arms. Sheila kissed her all over her face until her little girl giggled. Then she set her on a chair. "We might as well have the cookies now. I'm not very hungry." After brushing Becca's hair back from her face,

Sheila went to the counter. She handed them each a cookie and then she sat.

"These are good!" Becca said, squirming in her chair.

Sullivan plucked her up and set her on his lap. Becca looked at him in adoration. She had never had a man in her life. Neither of them had. Sheila was out of words. Being grateful for this moment with Becca so happy was how she should feel. But she didn't.

He'd leave them one day, and she'd have to explain things to Becca. She was too young to understand, but her heart would feel it. He was too close to them. How was she supposed soothe Becca's broken heart when her own heart hurt and she didn't have any words for herself? The hurt was a reminder she knew better. Her whole life had changed.

That evening, after Becca was in bed, Sheila stared into the flames, watching the wood burn brightly in colors of yellow, orange, and red. She needed to make a plan. She couldn't stay here. She never thought they'd be here more than a few days.

Lord, please show me the way. I'm trying to have a grateful heart, but I'm losing. It's a battle I don't know how to fight. I don't want to grow bitter and old before my time. If You might help me change my fate... I know the women in my family have had the same story and mine has been the same until now. Ultimately, it's Your choice, but a different town would be the best. I could work as a nurse, perhaps. I wish I had enough faith to just give You all my worries and know that it will all be fine. I have a lot of faith, but not enough. My worst flaw, but maybe I could change?

What would it be like to have hopes and dreams? She was grateful for the way her life had been. Letting out a shaky breath, she pulled her gaze from the flames and glanced at Sullivan to find him staring at her. His eyes were full of concern and she didn't blame him. She was concerned about herself too.

"I need a solid plan. Perhaps if it was just me this wait and see approach would be fine, but I have responsibilities. I need to rebuild or go to another town. I don't have the resources to do either, but the root cellar is probably still intact. That could be our shelter. There is almost always food to be had in nature. The root cellar has food I had put up in jars." She paused as a troubling thought occurred to her. "Oh, but the heat from the fire might have spoiled things. Maybe there are still some things growing in the garden. People lived that way before."

"What happens if it snows and you can't get out of the cellar?"

"We just stay inside until we can get out."

"You might not have enough air to survive."

She nodded. "I thought about that, and I'll figure something out. If I can't make that work, there is a cave not too far away that we can use. I am a child of God, and I am one with nature. I can survive. It'll be hard. I'm not fooling myself thinking it will be easy. I just need to make it safe for Becca and me to return to our land. Tomorrow I will see the sheriff."

HE WAS QUIET FOR A WHILE. He had nothing to say that she'd be happy to hear. "If things were fair and right, your plan would be a good one, a sound one. I know you're strong enough to survive, but I'm not sure the sheriff can help you. You don't have any witnesses that they're the ones who burned you out. Well, as of last week anyway. Things could have changed. If there aren't witnesses, the sheriff won't put any man in jail. But they might try to put you in jail because Jenny is dead."

The fear in her eyes tore at him, but he couldn't let her go back unless she knew every danger. "The men you'd accuse are men who live in our community. If it had been a band of outlaws, there would have been a posse chasing them, but it wasn't, and you may never get justice. Our winters aren't particularly hard like some places, but there have been years when it'd been particularly cold, and you'd be taking a huge chance. Becca might not make it through."

She sat back in the chair and closed her eyes as though she was in agony. He took her hand in his. "I'll help all I can. The best thing would be for you and Becca to live on the ranch."

"No. I refuse to be one of the strays your family takes in. You are all generous, but I wouldn't be able to look at myself in the mirror if I did that. I will find a way." She swallowed hard.

"What were you just thinking?"

She stared at the floor. "I was thinking I'll end up marrying someone and that would kill my soul, but I'd do it for Becca."

"It would really kill your soul?"

Bringing her head up, she stared into his eyes. "Yes, I think it would. Any man would expect a husbandly relationship and I'd feel obligated, but I'd hate myself every time. Plus, no man would put up with my ways. I'll have to come up with a new plan, won't I?" She sighed. "I'm exhausted. Sleep well."

He automatically turned his back so she could have privacy to change. So she'd marry another and probably end up dead for lack of protection. No one else would understand her need to wander the forests the way he did. She'd shrivel. How could she be herself in a gilded cage? Was it even possible? Hopefully one of his brothers would have good news for them soon.

He'd just decided he'd made a mistake allowing his horses

to go back to the ranch when Quinn arrived two days later. He had a doll for Becca, but she hid behind Sullivan the whole time while peeking at the doll Sullivan now had in his hands.

"Any news?" Sullivan asked.

"Not really. We went and cleared out the property so you can rebuild, Sheila. Heaven and the kids helped to harvest your garden. Ciara jarred what she could and dried some of the stuff. Gemma can hardly get out of a chair, but she helped too. Dolly is sewing some new things for Becca. She made the doll. We'd all feel better if you all came to the ranch." Quinn glanced between both Sheila and Sullivan. "I was told by Gemma that if you for some ridiculous reason decided not to come back, she would drive a wagon out here herself to come get you."

Sullivan's lips twitched until he saw the expression on Sheila's face. It almost looked like betrayal. She seemed shocked and her eyes were full of hurt.

"There is no way to refuse," she said tonelessly. She turned and looked out the window.

Quinn cocked his brow and Sullivan shrugged in return.

"I'm glad that's settled. We'll be here tomorrow to help you move. No one even knew you were gone, Sullivan. Donnell rode Zealous everywhere and most know your horse. He kept his distance, so most probably thought he was you."

Sullivan watched Sheila while he tried to keep track of what Quinn was saying.

"I'll be off." With a nod to them both, Quinn quietly left.

"Sully can I have the dolly?" Becca's dark eyes were wide with hope.

"Sure darlin'," he said as he gave her the doll. He bent and gave her a kiss on the cheek.

Becca smiled brightly before she climbed onto the bed

and examined her doll. Sheila still stood motionless at the window.

"Sheila?"

She turned and wrapped her arms around her middle.

———————

THIS WHOLE THING had made her weak. She hastily wiped away the few tears that had fallen. "Your family is taking on too much."

"They just want to help," he said gently.

"They have everything in motion without even a word to me. It's me that makes the decisions for my girl and me, not you and not your family. Maybe I decided to move on? But they cleared everything away to rebuild. Did they pick out plans for the house too? How many bedrooms are they building me? And they ravaged my garden. I have recipes I use when canning and I have my own way of drying herbs." She was trying to keep her voice down, but it was hard. "They all went too far. Your whole family is just like you!" Wide-eyed, she clasped her hands over her mouth.

Sullivan stared at her and turned away. It hurt that he'd put his back to her. It had been such a struggle to keep herself together these last weeks. He didn't turn around to face her, and it was her own fault; she'd been unyielding in her stubbornness. Her shoulders slumped. She was like Sullivan, and she'd been fighting him at every step. He wasn't right trying to fix everything for her, but she might have been more grateful and a whole less annoyed.

Oh Lord, how do I ask for forgiveness without it sounding as though I'm giving in to him? I don't want him to leave me.

He flinched when she lightly touched his back.

"Sullivan I'm going to put Becca to bed. I hope after that

we can talk. My emotions are turning me into someone I don't know anymore. Please Sullivan?"

He turned and looked into her eyes. She winced at the hurt and pain she saw in his blue eyes.

"How about I tell Becca a story while you get her ready for bed? I won't even turn around. I know a woman needs her privacy." He sidestepped Sheila and went to the bed where Becca had stood. She jumped into his arms and smiled before she buried her face in his neck. He held her close for a while and then set her down on the floor. "Get your nightgown."

Becca laughed and ran to a hook where her gown hung. She jumped but couldn't get it. Sullivan took it down and handed it to her. She handed it back.

"Mama will help you." He smiled at her.

"Sully help me."

The frightened expression on his face was priceless.

"Sully will start his story. I'll help you so we can listen." Sheila bit the bottom of her lip before she took the gown from him. Her heart felt heavy ; she'd ruined their friendship.

He reached out and cupped Sheila's cheek, and for a moment his eyes softened. Hope stirred. Perhaps she hadn't ruined things.

Sullivan finished his story while sitting on one side of the bed with Becca in the middle. She sat up and shook her head.

"What? You didn't like my story?"

"Sully, where is that bear from?"

"From? Why the woods, of course."

"A blue bear?" Becca shook her head at him.

"Bears aren't blue?" he asked.

"Nope," she said seriously. She gave him a sad frown. "Mama tell him."

"Sullivan, I don't know how to break this to you, but bears are usually brown. Sometimes I get colors wrong too."

"Me too," Becca said. "Don't be sad."

He reached over and hugged the young girl. "I appreciate you telling me the truth. Now I know that bears are brown. That fact will be useful to me."

Becca beamed as she put her head back on the pillow. Her eyes closed immediately.

Sheila hesitated by the bed. She rarely had to admit to people she had been wrong. This would not be easy. She sat on the empty chair in front of the fire, then lowered her head and stared at the ashes.

"I'm sorry, Sullivan. I shouldn't have said all those things about your family. I'm very sorry I insulted you. You've done so much for me and so has your family." She glanced up and met his gaze. "I'm so used to doing everything alone that I don't know how to accept help. I don't trust people anymore. I always think there is some motive in any kindness. I was carefree as a child. My mother said I had spunk. After the incident that left me pregnant, I changed, and when my mother died I changed even more." She looked away again. She probably disgusted him.

The next thing she knew she was being picked up into the air and then set back down on Sullivan's warm lap. His arms around her melted her frozen heart. He made her feel safe; as though everything would be just fine. He pulled her close to him and rested his chin on her head.

"Sullivan, can you forgive me?" she whispered.

"Honey, there's nothing to forgive. We all say things we don't mean. I'm glad you didn't mean them. Frankly, a few of the things you've said have hurt me, but I bet I've said things you didn't like either."

She'd hurt him? He was so big and tall and a man. Her words had more power than she thought. She'd have to think before she said no and rattled off the reasons.

"I thought I lost you."

He kissed the top of her head. "You can't get rid of me that easily. Have you ever talked to anyone about what happened with that man? I'm not asking you to tell me now, but if you want to, I'm here to listen. Sometimes it helps to talk about things."

She shivered. She'd rather not remember what happened. "Maybe someday. Where will we go tomorrow? Will you drop Becca and me at my place?"

He stilled. "Do you want me to drop you there?"

"I don't think I'd feel safe unless I had a door to lock. But I don't want to impose—"

He cut her off by lifting her chin and kissing her. It was a brief kiss, a tender kiss, and an unexpected kiss, but she could feel the powerful emotions behind it. When had this happened? She leaned against him, not wanting to run, and not wanting to encourage. Their truce was so new.

"Tomorrow will be a long day. I'd best get some sleep," she whispered as she slipped off his lap. Their gazes met, and for a moment there was nothing else in her life but him. Quickly she got herself together and broke the stare.

She turned, and as she walked to the bed, she heard a soft "Good night."

CHAPTER SIX

Sullivan watched as Sheila tried not to explode. All day she hadn't been given any choices. She was given clothes for her and Becca that she hadn't picked, and since they had already been hanging, she hadn't even been able to decide in which order to put them in the wardrobe.

"Now this mattress is big enough for you and Becca," Dolly said. "And I had the bed pushed against the wall so you can sleep on the outside and keep Becca from falling out."

Sheila stiffened but nodded without saying a word. It must be hard to be told what side of the bed to sleep on...as though it mattered to anyone else where she laid her head. He could tell she was grateful, but she'd bitten her lower lip almost raw.

"Tomorrow I'll order wood for the house. I was thinking that the house could be made bigger if you like," Donnell told her as he put a paper with the plans, he'd drawn in front of her. "I was thinking because there isn't much land to build on, we could build up. A two-story house is always nice. You'd have quite a view."

Sullivan knew she wasn't paying attention. Becca was at

Quinn and Heaven's house for the day, and she seemed to find it distracting.

"Maybe you should go over that tomorrow, Donnell, Sheila looks exhausted." Sullivan sat down next to her.

She gave him a lopsided smile and nodded. "I am weary, and I can't give your plan the attention it needs."

Sullivan put his hand over hers and she gave a sigh that could only have been one of relief.

"I think I'll take a walk." She pulled her hand away and hurried to the door.

Why was she racing so fast? Was she afraid she'd be told no? He had to admit she'd been treated more like a child than the woman she was for most of the day. She must be at the end of her rope. He'd give her a few minutes before he stepped outside to join her.

A cry rose from beyond the door. "No!"

Sullivan was out the door in a matter of seconds. He stopped and Dolly ran into his back. The sheriff was tying Sheila's hands in front of her. The two horses he had with him were skittish, dancing back and forth nervously.

"Wait!" Dolly shouted. "I'll get her wrap and bonnet for her."

The sheriff's expression soured, but he nodded.

Sullivan stepped closer. "Why are you taking her in?"

"You're lucky I'm not taking you too. It's against the law to hide a fugitive."

Sullivan reeled backward. "A fugitive?"

The sheriff gave a curt nod and spat on the ground. "She's charged with the murder of Jenny Wren and with running from the law."

Dolly came out with packed saddlebags. Then she put Sheila's bonnet on for her followed by her wrap. "I packed extra clothes and some things you'll need."

Sheila nodded, but her eyes held terror. "Becca…"

"She'll be safe," Dolly promised.

The sheriff moved to put his hands on her, and Sullivan pushed him aside with his shoulder. He touched her cheek briefly and then he put his hands around her thin waist, lifting her onto the saddle. Then he arranged her dress to cover as much of her legs as possible.

The sheriff grabbed the saddlebags and put them on the horse he'd rode. Then, clutching the reins of Sheila's horse in one hand, he mounted. He was having trouble controlling them both. He had no business with those two horses. And if he didn't take care, he would lose his grip on the reins. Sheila held on to the pommel, her knuckles white around it.

"You can visit in a day or two," said the sheriff. Then he spurred his mount forward. "Haw!"

———

HER HEART POUNDED WILDLY AS she bounced in the saddle, her tied hands preventing her from properly holding on. The sheriff couldn't control these horses. They were both going to meet their demise.

"Sheriff Ganes, please slow down!" she cried.

He paid no heed.

Her poor Becca. What would they tell her? Would she be sent away or would the Kavanaghs take her in? A warmth touched her. She already knew the answer, Sullivan would raise her as his own. But she still would be without a mother if Sheila didn't find a way out of her situation and return to her child.

She hung on, reliving the kiss she'd shared with Sullivan. She'd seen men kiss their wives on the forehead in a sweet manner, but she had never expected his kiss to be so tender. The heady feeling had coursed through her. His lips had been

45

gentle yet masculine. There hadn't been many such tender moments in her life except with Becca.

The town came into view, and she started to shake. The day would probably end with her hanged from a rope. In some ways she'd thought her life was just beginning. She'd wasted so much time being put out by Sullivan for his controlling ways. She should have told him what happened to her, and maybe he would have understood. Now talking to the sheriff would be like talking to the wind. The words would be gone before they were heard. She knew how to cure ailments, but she never figured out the curse part, so if she was a witch, she wasn't a very good one.

They were soon surrounded by a mob of people, screaming for justice. Would she even make it inside the jail? The sheriff's office door opened, and a burly young deputy pushed through and pulled her from the horse. He gripped her upper arm until the pain brought tears.

"I don't have all day. Get a move on!" He shoved her through the door, and she fell.

She lay on the cold slate floor for a moment to catch her breath. She tried to sit up, but the deputy put his foot on her shoulder and kept her down. The sheriff entered and snickered at her.

"Moore, let her up and throw her into the first cell there."

She was dragged more than she was helped up. The cell door opened with a loud creak. She hit the ground again, this time smashing her hip, and the door slammed behind her. It was a while before she managed to get up, her hands were stilled tied.

The tick mattress was heavily stained, and the smell of urine was overwhelming. She stood against the wall, hoping she'd be untied. So far, they'd ignored her and any questions she asked. That probably didn't bode well.

A crowd was gathering outside and plenty of them

shouted "hang the witch," while others wanted her burned at the stake. A shudder rippled through her. This wasn't supposed to be her fate, was it? What about Becca? Her poor baby must be scared.

"Could you please untie my hands?"

Sheriff Ganes shrugged, swung his feet off the desk, and stood. He made a big show of stretching before he grabbed the keys and a knife. The sneer on his face made her nervous.

"Put your hands out through the bars." As soon as she did, he cut the rope and grabbed her wrist. "I don't want any trouble, you hear?"

She nodded, wanting him to let go of her. Abruptly, he dropped her hands and walked back to his desk. She glanced at the other cells. They were empty, and they didn't look as filthy as hers. She'd operated on the sheriff once. It had been a long and difficult process, but she had gotten him up and back to work. Had all she'd done been for nothing? Dying didn't bother her as much as leaving Becca behind. It didn't matter how she was conceived; the moment she had seen her baby's face, Sheila had fallen in love.

It would have been nice to spend more time with Sullivan. He was a worthy man but that didn't mean he'd meant anything by his kiss. More than likely he'd felt sorry for her. Still, she would have liked to have seen if it could have led somewhere.

After pacing for a while, she found a small space that wasn't as dirty. She sat down on the cold floor and leaned back against the hard wall. It wasn't comfortable, but she hadn't planned on sleeping much anyway. The noise from the crowd outside didn't seem as loud, it seemed as it grew later more and more of them left.

Lord, I don't know what to say. I could plead for my life but I'm sure my life and death are already known to you. Please keep Becca safe and away from healing. I took too much pride in my ability to heal. I have my share of anger I can't seem to let go. I'm filled with too much doubt. All the things a good Christian should be, I've failed. I have faith in You, and I know You know best. That is why I'm not begging for my life. I have tried to keep myself modest and sin free. You know I've had so many offers over the years but none that were decent. Becca and I sometimes went without because I refused to go against my teachings as a Christian.

I've seen people flinch when I touch them. They don't think of me as having an ounce of virtue. For the most part I've held my tongue. I knew most folks wouldn't thank me or pay me, but I still went when asked. I figured my healing was a gift You gave to me and I was to share it. Lord, You know I didn't kill Jenny, and I don't want Becca to have to live with something I didn't do. It will be a millstone around her neck. Watch over her and keep her safe.

Thank you for sending Sullivan into my life. He was able to postpone the inevitable, and he showed me just how stubborn I am. I'm afraid to lean on anyone. I never could rely on anyone other than my ma. It's been safer to do things on my own. He's a good man and I hope that someday You will bring love into his heart. He'd be a wonderful husband and father. As I sit here, I will still have doubts. I can't help it. My doubts aren't about You but the other people. Bless me please, Lord. Amen.

SULLIVAN BRISTLED AS DOLLY PUSHED AHEAD of him. The sheriff had said to visit in a day or two, but the morning following Sheila being taken away, Dolly announced he had kept them away long enough. And now as they headed toward the jail door, she got there first and burst through, although he followed right on her heels. It took a few seconds for his eyes to adjust to the dim lighting, but when they did, he spotted Sheila lying on the floor against the wall. Fury flared, swift and hot.

"Oh no!" Dolly swept the sheriff's feet off his desk. "You expected Sheila to sleep on the floor? What kind of man are you?"

"There's a bed in there," he grumbled, rubbing his eyes.

Sullivan tempered his anger so he wouldn't punch the sheriff and end up behind bars himself. But it hurt to see Sheila behind bars and huddled on the floor. He hurried over to her and wrapped his hands around two bars as he peered through.

"Are you all right? I bet you didn't sleep all night. I know I didn't." He took a wilted flower out of his pocket and handed it to her. "Becca picked it for you. I thought it was getting to be too cold for flowers."

Her eyes swam as she took the flower. "How is my girl?"

"She misses you, but she's fine. Everyone has been keeping her busy."

She pressed her lips together as tears trailed down her face. "What will become of her once I'm dead?"

If only he could reach in and hold her. He put his hands over hers and squeezed. "You aren't going to die."

"I might," she said stoically. "And it must be faced. Becca needs seeing to."

"She'll be sent to an orphanage," the sheriff announced. His satisfied tone of voice made its way under Sullivan's skin.

"We'll keep her. I'll keep her and raise her. Don't worry." Sullivan had been so intent on Sheila he didn't realize Dolly's absence until she reentered the jailhouse with a mop and bucket.

"Sullivan, I purchased a whole bunch of stuff at the General Store."

"I'll get it Dolly." He smiled at Sheila, but his smile didn't feel real. He and his brothers had talked long into the night and had been unable to form a plan to get her out, and everyone he'd met on his way through town seemed out for blood.

He walked to the store and discovered Dolly had not lied when she'd said she bought a lot of supplies. He gathered what he could and returned to the jail carrying a new tick, a sheet and two blankets along with things to give Sheila's cell a good cleaning.

"Now wait a doggone minute! You can't go bringing your own things into the jail!" Sheriff Ganes' face turned a bright crimson. "There is nothing wrong with the way I keep the cells!"

"If you enjoy vermin then yes, you are doing a great job," Dolly said, her voice laced in sarcasm.

"Don't make me pull my gun on you." His eyes turned cold as he stood.

"Now, there's no reason to have your gun out," Sullivan said in a calm voice. "We're just going to make sure Miss. Kelly is comfortable. How long until the judge comes to town?"

"Three weeks. I sent a telegram, and three weeks is the best he could do." The sheriff unlocked the cell door.

Sullivan glanced at Sheila and her look of terror was like getting kicked in the gut. There had to be something he could do besides making her bed.

"What did Mrs. Wren have to say? The child was dead before she got to Miss. Kelly's place. I know they're grieving, but the truth needs to be told." He ran his hand over his jaw.

Ganes walked over to the fresh coffee Dolly had made and poured himself a cup. "Seems to me the best truth is what was said right after the incident. Jenny's pa insists she was alive and minutes later she was dead. It seems simple to me." He ambled over to his desk and sat down in his chair again.

"Did you even question Miss. Kelly? She has her side in all

of this." Sullivan couldn't keep his voice from growing louder, harsher.

But Ganes only shrugged. "Like I said, the judge will be here in three weeks. It's going to be her word against his, and likely the grieving father will win. Nothing else to do about it."

Sullivan closed his eyes for a moment, struggling once again to curb his urge to punch the sheriff. He helped Dolly put the new mattress in and take the old one out. Then he helped to make the bed, watching Sheila the whole time. He didn't like her deflated look. She was a fighter, but she sure wasn't acting like one. He picked her up and sat her on the cot.

He lifted her chin until their gazes met. "Don't give up. I'll get you out of here."

She glanced away. "I know you want me back at the ranch, but you just might have to accept that this isn't going your way." Her breathing hitched. "Dolly please give Becca lots of kisses and hugs from me. Tell her—" Her voice broke. "Tell her Mama loves her." A sob erupted and Sheila covered her mouth with her hands.

Dolly handed her a Bible and kissed her cheek. "Don't you worry about Becca."

"Thank you."

Dolly took the mop, broom, and bucket and placed them in a corner of the office.

He caressed Sheila's face. "Do you remember what I said about you can't get rid of me easily?"

She nodded.

"I'll be back tomorrow. I have a few telegrams of my own to send, and then I'll spend time with Becca. Hang in there." He kissed her cheek before he walked out of the cell. She looked so lost it scared him.

CHAPTER SEVEN

*O*ver the next couple of weeks, Sheila's emotions changed quickly, and after a visit with Becca she felt particularly low. Becca begged to stay with her. It'd hurt too much to see her. Sheila never felt so hopeless. The judge was due to arrive in under a week. All she'd ever wanted was to be a good person and raise her daughter. She was still a good person, but few would agree. Donnell had been intent on getting her house built before she was released. She wasn't being consulted, and she didn't much care. What would it matter, if she was not alive to enjoy it?

All the Kavanaghs had been by to see her at some point. Gemma had her baby and thankfully Doctor Bright was there to attend her. She'd had a healthy girl, and Gemma and Teagan named her Lacey. It had been torture to sit in the cell when Shea rode in to get the doctor. It'd seemed like forever before she'd gotten the good news.

Ed Wren had slammed into the jail afterwards, sneering at her. He'd told her the Kavanaghs were lucky she was locked up and couldn't harm their new baby. Even though it was a lie, it cut her to the core. She hadn't stuck up for herself, hadn't said anything, in fact. It wouldn't have changed anything, and certainly not the man's opinion of her.

She'd hated relying on folks, but that was all she could do. Shivering, she pulled one of her blankets tighter around her shoulders. The sheriff never put wood in the stove when he did his rounds and then went to the saloon at night. The only thing that saved her from freezing to death was John O'Rourke sneaking in each night to put enough wood on to heat the place. Ciara's sister Orla spent many hours with her. She would hold up a blanket so Sheila could dress behind it each day when she was brought clean clothes.

But her biggest concern was what would happen to Becca? The sheriff and Ed Wren were insistent that she'd go to the state orphanage. They said the Kavanaghs had no legal right to keep her. Time was running out.

The door opened, and Reverend McKay walked into the jail, smiling at her. "It's good to see you, Sheila. I thought I would be late, but the other party isn't here yet."

Confusion clouded her thoughts. "Other party?"

The door opened again, admitting Sullivan and Angus.

"There they are." Reverend McKay beamed. "We should probably get this done before the sheriff or his deputy get back from lunch. Sullivan, stand next to Sheila as close as the bars allow you."

What was going on? She looked between all three men. Her body shook.

"Dearly beloved..." Those were the only words she heard over the buzzing in her ears. She glanced from Sullivan to Angus to the reverend, and still she did not understand what they were doing.

"Sheila, you need to sign this," the reverend told her after a fashion.

She studied the piece of paper and was stunned. She

signed it and handed it back to the reverend. Then she sat on her cot. No one had asked her if she wanted to be married. It must be her punishment for being so stubborn and argumentative. She had thought she knew what was right, and now she was being shown in all kinds of horrible ways that she had no control over her life. She watched in silence as the reverend and Angus left, and then she stared at Sullivan.

At least he looked uncomfortable. "Now Becca can stay with me. No one will take a girl away from her family."

Sheila lay down on the cot and turned her back to him. It was all too much, and she'd never been so overwhelmed before. It was as though she was watching someone else's life. She would never have allowed this to happen.

"Sheila? Everything will be fine."

She nodded but didn't turn around. It would all be over in a matter of days. Suddenly, she sat up and swung her legs over the side of the bed. "I want to see Becca before…" A lump of emotion tightened her throat and kept her from finishing the sentence.

"I'll bring her tomorrow," he blurted. "We can explain our marriage together."

She stared at him, shaking her head. "I'd like someone to explain it all to me. I'm the one with death hanging over my head, and I haven't been asked one thing. I wasn't even asked if I wanted to marry you. I think you did it for Becca's sake, but why couldn't you have talked to me about it? You all are acting as though I'm already dead. My feelings or opinions don't matter one bit." Her heart hammered in her chest. Calming herself would not be easy, but she needed to be calm to accept God's will.

The sheriff raced in. His face was flushed, and he was out of breath. "Is it true? You got married?" His dark eyes glittered, and his demeanor terrified her.

"Yes. Sheila is my wife."

"But it has to be consummated!"

Sullivan smiled wide and opened his hand. He held the key to the cell. "Don't worry we know how it all works. I'll be back tomorrow, my love."

Was she going crazy? What was going on? Lies slid too easily off Sullivan's tongue. He wasn't a man she could trust. Once again, she'd judged a man's character wrong. She lay back down with her back to them.

The sheriff left in a huff. But she had no time to wonder where he was going as the door opened and closed again as soon as he left.

"I was hoping to catch you alone."

A shiver went up her spine as panic swept through her. She knew that voice. It had haunted her for over five years. It was the voice of her nightmares. She didn't bother to turn around. She didn't want to see him.

"I'm taking our daughter home with me after the trial. Your sham marriage got you nothing. No Kavanagh is going to raise my child."

"Do you even know the name of your child?" she asked coldly. "Do you know if it's a boy or girl? What does this child look like? Are you finally admitting to raping me?" Her voice was bitter, but it couldn't be helped.

"I remember having a good ol' time with you. Force hadn't been needed. The sheriff just told me about the girl. My daughter will live with me and my ma. I will make sure the girl never tries to heal anything."

Sheila could hardly breathe. "Why? I always wondered why it was me you raped."

"Your big brown eyes were begging for it, and I obliged." With that, she heard his footsteps shuffle across the floor as he left, slamming the door behind him.

She reached for her bible and read Psalm 23.

The LORD is my shepherd; I shall not want.

He maketh me to lie down in green pastures: he leadeth me beside the still waters.

He restoreth my soul: he leadeth me in the paths of right-eousness for his name's sake.

Yea, though I walk through the valley of the shadow of death, I will fear no evil: for thou art with me; thy rod and thy staff they comfort me.

Thou preparest a table before me in the presence of mine enemies: thou anointest my head with oil; my cup runneth over.

Surely goodness and mercy shall follow me all the days of my life: and I will dwell in the house of the LORD for ever.

The verses comforted her, but not because she expected to die. To her, they meant that God was always with her. Sadness washed over her, but she had no more tears to cry. Sullivan would have to keep Becca protected, and that she knew he could do. She'd discuss it with him like normal people.

SNUGGLING TOGETHER, Sheila and Becca made a beautiful picture. Sullivan hadn't noticed before just how much mother and daughter looked alike. Sheila's eyes spoke of happiness, but he could see the pain behind them. It was getting too crowded and rowdy in the town to bring Becca back. They were jostled on the short walk from the wagon to the jail. It would only get worse.

Arranging their marriage without asking her was unfor-giveable, but he wasn't sorry he'd done it. Sheila stirred him. She warmed his heart in a way he never imagined, and just like that, in the blink of an eye, he could lose her. He swallowed hard when Sheila gazed at him over her daughter's head. He read a bit of resignation in her. He'd much rather be sparring with her than see her defeated.

She rocked with Becca's head on her shoulder. "I had a visitor yesterday. He is someone who came into my life over five years ago. He said he had a claim here, and it didn't matter about our wedding ceremony. I need to know you can... actually I'm asking you to protect her against that claim. She is the thing most precious to me, and I can't be in peace if he gets his way."

"He was here?"

She nodded as she continued to rock back and forth.

"Don't worry, but I won't be here for the trial. I'll be making tracks."

A few tears spilled down her face. "I'd hoped you'd agree. Thank you from the bottom of my heart."

"I've been praying things go your way." He couldn't even summon a smile for her. His heart was splintering.

"I thought you didn't believe in God."

He shrugged. "I counted my many blessings and realized God had always been with me."

The sheriff returned to his office. "Visitin' hours are over."

He was lying, of course. There were no set hours for visiting, never had been. But Sullivan didn't want to make things worse for Sheila. How was he supposed to take her child from her? Steeling himself against his sadness, he bent and gently cradled the sleeping girl in his arms. Before straightened up, his lips found Sheila's. The kiss was all too brief. He whispered into her ear. "I love you so much." He couldn't look her in the eye; he was afraid he'd break down and that could tip the sheriff off to his plan.

"Sullivan?" He stopped but didn't turn back to her. "My heart breaks when we say goodbye. Please for my sake stay away."

He nodded and walked out of her life.

He wanted to rage at the world, but he had to stay calm

for Becca's sake. Riding to the ranch using the long way home, he stopped at the back door. He slid out of the saddle with the small girl in his arms. Quietly, he entered the house and handed a sleeping Becca to Dolly.

"I'm going to pack a few things for me and Becca and then take off. The scum that sired her plans to take her once Sheila is sentenced. I don't think she will be, but if things go wrong, I have an army buddy in Oklahoma." He let out a shaky breath.

"You're a fine man Sullivan, and I'm proud of you," Dolly told him.

His heart warmed briefly at her praise. "I'll be back in a few." He headed upstairs to grab some clothes. He took a moment and sat on Sheila's bed, holding her pillow to him. It smelled like lavender. He was going to miss her more than he ever thought possible, but he hoped the lawyer he hired would arrive today and get her out of jail. Ben Whittaker was another army friend, and he was good. He always dressed like a dusty cowhand and enjoyed being underestimated.

"I'll keep your daughter safe," he said in the empty room. He hurried to pack supplies while Donnell hitched the wagon.

Becca cried when she woke up. It broke his heart to watch her peer around for her mother. Dolly tried to soothe her, but it wasn't until she was back in Sullivan's arms that she quieted. He wanted to get out of there before the whole family gathered.

"Donnell knows how to get in touch with me and he also knows the lawyer I hired. Take care of my,... my love until I can come back for her." He skedaddled to the wagon and put Becca on the seat and then sat next to her. He put his arm around her and held the reins.

A TALL, handsome cowboy with blond hair entered the jail-house. The sheriff scowled at him.

"What do you want?" he asked irritably.

"I'm here to visit Mrs. Kavanagh. I'm her lawyer." He stuck out his hand. "Ben Whittaker is the name."

Sheriff Ganes looked at Ben's hand and ignored it. "Where do you hale from?"

"I mostly drift around Texas. Sullivan Kavanagh hired me, and I'd like to talk to my client in private."

Ganes looked the man up and down. "I can let you in her cell. Keep your voice down and that's as private as it gets."

Sheila's eyes widened. This was the man who was to defend her? Her stomach clenched. She was as good as dead. She tried to smile at him when he entered her cell. She shook his hand and invited him to sit on the cot with her.

"I'll need a bit of background. Were you and Sullivan in a close relationship when this happened?"

"He'd been to visit a few times."

"It was more like courting you and not an affair?"

Sheila drew in a swift breath. "It was neither. We were just friends. There weren't flowers or candy and we never rode in a buggy to have a picnic. I think he liked to talk to me. The war wasn't gentle on anyone."

"You had your daughter out of wedlock, did you not?"

She frowned. "Yes, yes I did. I was attacked and the result was my daughter."

"Able Langton's child, correct?"

She gave a start. How on earth did he know that? "Listen, if this is how you ask questions, then you can leave. I won't be insulted by you or anyone else."

"These are the same questions you'll be asked in court," he said, meeting her gaze with his clear blue eyes, "and I need to know what the answers are so I can help you."

"Are you sure you know what you're doing? You're

dressed like a cowboy back from a cattle drive, though you talk like a well-educated man. Just how do you know Sullivan?"

He nodded. "Sullivan and I served together in the army. He saved my life a few times."

A sigh slipped out. "That sounds like him."

Ben Whittaker chuckled his agreement. "He likes to be the protector of everyone."

Protector, that was a good word for Sullivan. She'd mull it over later.

"So, what I know is Ed Wren brought his daughter into town first. The doctor wasn't here, and he came to you. He's claiming it was a bad cough and you gave her poison."

Her jaw dropped. The lies got bigger and bigger. "He says he rode to town with Jenny because of a cough? Why didn't he send one of the men to get the doctor? Mr. Whittaker, this is the first I've heard of a cough."

"Call me Ben."

"I'm Sheila." Frustration made her edgy. "Ben, Jenny's body was badly burned, and the poor child must have suffered dearly making the trip to town and then to my place. She'd been dressed in nice clothes and just doing that, changing her clothes must have been excruciating. I don't know if she was given anything for the pain. But she was dead when Ed Wren carried her inside. I no sooner told him I was sorry that I couldn't help before someone shouted 'witch.' I grew fearful for my life, and I ran and was chased by the men he brought."

"How many men did he bring?"

"At least four that I could see," she answered. "Behind my house there is nothing but woods, and I've spent time in them since I could walk. I knew the trails and I had hoped to get to the Kavanagh Ranch."

"I see."

"Becca and I were reunited at the ranch house. We hid in a cabin for a while and they burned my house down. Then we moved back to the Kavanagh ranch and soon enough the sheriff came and got me, brought me here. Sullivan married me thinking he would have a legal right to Becca, but her real father who has never even seen her came here declaring his intent to take my daughter." She leaned toward him, hoping he would understand the importance of her next words. "I don't want to hang, but I'd rather you keep Able Langton from getting her than waste time defending me. I just want my daughter safe."

Ben stood. "I have enough background to start. Seems odd to me that no one saw Jenny in town that day. I would have thought it would be something everyone remembered. I'm sure there was shouting and panic. I've seen men severely burned in the war and touching them brought too much pain." He shuddered. "Those who could make a sound... screamed with the agony. Seems to me, if she wasn't screaming, maybe she was already dead. Maybe even before they dressed her." He nodded to her. "It was nice to meet you, Mrs. Kavanagh. I'll be back." He waited by the cell door, his face showing no expression, while Ganes took his time shuffling over with the key.

CHAPTER EIGHT

The trial was to be tomorrow, and the gallows were already being built right outside her cell window. The town must be confident she would be convicted. She had complete faith, and that faith had gotten her through all the days of her life. If she was to hang, then she'd have to accept it. With her faith, though, came an abundance of pain. She'd never see Becca's first day at school or her wedding. She'd never see her grandchildren. She'd miss so many important moments. Would Sullivan marry again? He might just find love. It was a gift she'd experienced; a love that ran deep. Why couldn't she be more like her mother, accepting of everything with a smile on her face?

She crawled onto her bed, stood, and looked out the window. Of course, Ed Wren and his boys were all helping to build the gallows. She'd never heard of anyone hanging from a gallows in these parts before. Many took justice into their own hands. Horse thieves were often hanged from the nearest tree. If a person had witnesses everything was fine, she supposed. Too bad she had none. She'd probably draw a big crowd. It would be good for the town businesses.

There was always a silver lining, though, if folks just took time to look for it. Movement at the edge of the crowd building the gallows caught her attention, and she gasped. Able was out there with his hammer swinging away. *He* deserved to be hanged for what he'd done to her. She'd avoided men all the years since, except for her friendship with Sullivan. She'd never have made a good wife. There was no way she'd sleep in the same bed as a man. Not that she would have to worry about doing that, she realized. Despair engulfed her. It was hard acting brave when she was afraid of her own shadow.

The Lord had sent Sullivan to look out for Becca, and for that she was forever grateful. At least once Sheila was dead, she'd be free of her excruciating heartbreak. Should she tell Sullivan how she loved him so? Would it make things harder for him? Perhaps. Or maybe he could carry her love in his heart for a while.

She never had gotten a chance to see Gemma and Teagan's baby. There would be plenty of babies born on that ranch. Life would go on without her. Sullivan wouldn't come around; she'd asked him not to, but now regretted that. His reassuring smile would have been wonderful.

She climbed down and curled up on the cot. If she was home, she'd have a good cry, a loud cry. But she wasn't home. So many things raced through her mind. Sullivan knew to try to break the cycle of the women in her family, didn't he? She never wanted Becca to suffer at the hands of any man. Did he know she was afraid of thunder?

CHAPTER NINE

*S*heila's palms were sweaty, and her legs barely supported her body as she walked between the sheriff and another man she didn't know. This was it. Her fate would be declared in the saloon of all places, since the town didn't have a proper courthouse. She took a deep breath of freedom. It could be her last. As she was wound through the loud crowd, hands reached out and her hair and dress were pulled. The sheriff acted as though he didn't notice. Nary a hopeful face was to be seen.

She knew she had shadows under her eyes. She hadn't slept all night. She mourned her daughter. She mourned life. It would go on without her, but it was hard to know that once she was gone, that was that. She'd left no lasting impression in the world, nothing to be remembered for. Oh, people would probably talk about the witch that was hanged for a good many years, but that was the kind of remembering she didn't want. She had always tried to live her life in God's light. It had been a good, understanding, comforting light.

They entered the saloon, and it appalled her to see the bartender serving drinks. She was fighting for her life, and it was entertainment for them. Her hands shook. This was bound to be over quickly. Men who worked for Ed Wren took most of the chairs. Then she saw Teagan and his brothers and Dolly. When she got to the front, she saw Able with a sneer on his face. If it had been possible, she would have run.

Sullivan wasn't supposed to be there, he'd told her as much. But her heart cried out for his. She needed him. How was she supposed to remain calm without him? A sense of panic went through her. She sat at a table next to her lawyer, Ben. Thank goodness he seemed confident.

She watched as one man after another told the judge she was a witch who had killed Jenny. Hearing such things made her die a little inside with each testimony. She needed Sullivan to hold her hand. How soon after a verdict did, they hang people? Would she ever see him again?

Jumping up and crying liar wasn't allowed, but she wanted to do it. Her heart broke at the words she heard. Why hadn't she known that people hated her? Why had they come to her if they hated her so?

Ben gave her some hope. He asked questions that made some witnesses seem dim-witted and others downright liars. A few of the men who took the stand hadn't even been in town during the time this all happened. He made some great points.

Sheila glanced around but didn't see Ed Wren's wife. Why wasn't she here?

Finally, it was her turn to take the stand. She told the truth, but she didn't have any reason to think the judge believed her. Was he even paying attention? He had certainly seemed interested when Ed Wren told his lies, sitting and watching the man intently. Ben was able to get in his theory that Jenny was already dead when she got to Sheila's.

Sheila testified that the child was burned, and Ed had

said she had a cough. Sheila's stomach roiled; it was awful to be accused of something she had never done. Telling the truth meant nothing to these people who were drinking whiskey. She was fighting for her life and they were getting drunk.

Mrs. Wren was called, and she shuffled in. Sheila had seen her before, but now she looked like a shell of that woman. Mrs. Wren sat in the chair next to the judge and stared with an unfocused gaze. She looked to be drugged.

Ben stood. "Mrs. Wren, how was your daughter injured?"

"Jenny?" She glanced around, clearly confused.

"Yes Jenny. Did she get burned by the fire?"

She nodded. "It was a horrible thing, the screams, the smell." Then she shook her head. "She had a cough."

"Mrs. Wren, was Jenny alive when she was taken to the doctor?"

"She wasn't feeling any pain. I was able to put new clothes on her. Her skin came off in sheets when I took her burned clothes off her. I'll never forget it." Mrs. Wren glanced at her red-faced husband. "She had a cough."

"Has Sheila Kavanagh been to your house to tend to you before?" Ben asked.

"Why, yes. I rather have a female looking at me than a man." A ghost of a smile appeared on her face as she glanced at Sheila. "I didn't know you got married, Sheila. Congratulations! Which of the Kavanaghs is yours?"

"She is married to Sullivan," Ben said gently. Then he redirected her. "Were you told that Jenny was alive when she was brought to Sheila's house?"

Mrs. Wren looked confused again. "She had a cough, but then she was silent. Ed promised to make her better, and he rode away with her and many of his men. My arms were so empty. I went inside to decide what she'd be buried in."

A loud cough came from the area where Mr. Wren sat.

"She had a cough," Mrs. Wren repeated in a weak voice. "I'm telling them what you told me, Ed, she had a cough."

"I'm very sorry for your loss, Mrs. Wren," Ben said.

"We buried her in a beautiful blue gown that made her look like a princess. I had to find long gloves to hide how bad the burns on her arms were."

"I have no further questions." Ben sat back down.

Next, Alicia Goren was called.

"You work for Dr. Bright don't you Miss. Goren?" asked Ben.

"Yes, I do. I'm his nurse."

"Were you the one who told Mr. Wren that Dr. Bright wasn't in?"

She hesitated. "Yes."

"The doctor was in his office, wasn't he?" Ben pressed.

Alicia shifted in her seat. "There wasn't anything the doctor could have done. I checked the girl's pulse. And she had already died. I tried to tell Mr. Wren, but he refused to believe me, so I sent him to Sheila's place. I figured she could deal with him."

"Can you tell me why you didn't come forward before this? Mrs. Kavanagh has sat in a cell for weeks now."

She shifted in her seat. "It—it wasn't any of my business."

Doctor Bright stood and walked out of the saloon. Alicia's shoulders slumped; she looked as though she'd lost her best friend.

Sheila didn't pay too much attention after that. That woman had known she was innocent but never said a word. Sheila's spirit felt bruised. It wasn't her business? How? Why? Who did that? Who didn't help another when it was within their power to help? This was a life or death situation! People really had such cold hearts? She'd been betrayed at every turn... and for what? It was an accident that had killed poor Jenny. The world had gone crazy, and she was in the center of it. She couldn't put her trust in anyone ever again. She might never get a chance. Her serene feeling of it being fine if she died was replaced by fury. Sheila felt more alive than she ever had. Her fate was in the hands of the judge, and she didn't trust him to do the right thing. A person should be able to trust a judge, the sheriff, and witnesses. She was better than all of them combined.

Ben put his arm around her and helped her to stand. Everyone was silent as they waited for the judge to announce the verdict.

"Guilty." The judge raised his gavel and brought it down hard on the table. "Her sentence is three years in the women's prison."

Sheila wanted to sag into the chair, but she stood up tall with her head held high. Every single person knew for a fact she wasn't guilty, yet there were no sounds of protest. She was immediately shackled, hands and legs, and hauled into a wagon. She fell against the side as they drove her out of town. Blood ran down her face.

Should she be looking for the silver lining? Should she be glad they didn't hang her but sentenced her to a slow death instead? She closed her eyes, but that didn't help the tears that poured out.

CHAPTER TEN

hree years later
They shoved Sheila out of the prison door. All they gave her was water and a bit of food. Other than that, she had on her threadbare prison dress, falling apart shoes, and a ripped scarf wrapped around her head.

No one was there to greet her or take her away. She'd already known that was how it would be. Sullivan had never written one letter. She still wrote him, hoping Becca was getting her letters, though Sheila never heard back. It took a moment for her to stand up straight. She'd aged at least twenty years while in prison.

The thought of going to the Kavanagh ranch made her sick, but she had to find out what had happened to Becca. She shuffled one foot then the other, heading north. There was a slim chance she'd make it, but she had to try.

She was glad of her skills as she traveled. She was able to find roots to grind together for pain, and she knew how to make a fire. She even snagged a few rabbits and some fish. She stayed as close to the various streams as she could and even found a few treasures along the way; a cup, a pot, and a piece of a mirror.

Perhaps the mirror wasn't a treasure, she thought as she stared at her reflection. Her once shiny dark hair was now dull and thin. She tried to smile, but it felt too foreign to her. Her bones jutted out and she had a hideous scar on the side of her face just under her jaw. No one had cared when she had been injured. She'd had to beg for a needle and thread to sew it up herself. It surprised her she could still go on.

She had helped as many as she could while serving her sentence. Few made it to the end of their stay in that prison. There was no room for niceness. Only the strong survived by making sure they got the food and water allotted to them. Some took more than their share. Everyone was on their own in there. It did no good to make friends, people died too quickly. There were lice and rats, and still no one cared.

They took away bibles from those who had them. It was hard to find God in there. She'd felt forsaken more than once. She'd had so much faith, but it didn't survive in there. So many died and the survivors had to bury them. It had been a place of despair, and how she made it out she had no idea. Still, she shuffled on.

Her shoes were attached to her feet by pieces of tied cloth. She was cold, she was always cold it seemed, and she covered herself in dry leaves at night. It helped some. All that mattered was Becca. She'd decided not to disrupt her life. It must be hard trying to grow up with everyone knowing your ma was in prison. If she was safe and happy, Sheila would move on. But first she had to find out.

Her mind returned to thoughts of the prison. She'd never known men could be so brutal, but somehow, she had survived. A few of the women went mad, and they were killed. Everywhere, every day there was the threat of being shot. Then there was constant sickness and no medicine.

She wished she had happy things to fill her thoughts as she shuffled along, but nothing came to mind. Her heart was still in shreds after the years in prison, and it refused to heal. What she would do after she saw Becca, she had no idea. Ex-convicts weren't welcome in any place she could think of. But it didn't matter, she would willingly die as long as she knew about Becca.

Did Becca have a new mother? Had Sullivan found a new wife and had he kept her daughter? Perhaps if Sheila could get enough food to make her look normal... No, it wouldn't matter, she was unwanted. Becca would be going to school by now. Her one prayer had been that Able hadn't gotten ahold of her. But were her prayers even heard anymore?

There was so much bitterness inside of her. There would never be a normal life for her. She couldn't bring herself to care for or trust anyone. After weeks of walking, she recognized landmarks. When she came to the familiar stream, although it was chilly, she undressed and walked into the water. She couldn't remember when she had been clean last. She reached down and used sand and pebbles to clean herself. A sliver of soap would have been a luxury, but even the clean water was something she'd never expected to have again while she was in prison.

The fire was built up nice and high to keep her warm and to dry her. The closer she got to Kavanagh land, the more she dreamed of her precious daughter. In some dreams she was happy, and in some she suffered. Tomorrow she'd be at the Kavanagh ranch. As she remembered it, there were plenty of trees surrounding the home, and she'd be able to watch them from afar.

SULLIVAN SMILED AT GAIL. She'd been a godsend this last year. The bright sun showed off the highlights in her dark hair, and her blue eyes were calm. He'd wanted calm and simple. She'd looked after Becca for him. Dolly had done it at first when he couldn't take Becca with him, but with a few toddlers running around it was just too much for her.

He swallowed hard. He couldn't think about Becca without mourning Sheila. He'd miss his love for the rest of his life. People told him that time would take care of his pain, but it hadn't. He carried the ache within him, and it was as strong now as the day they had been notified of her death. She was buried in an unmarked grave on the prison property, they had been informed, and visitors were not permitted. People naturally thought that he and Gail… but he didn't feel that way.

Becca ran out of the house, her long braids trailing behind her. A brown dog named Hugs followed her, making the little girl laugh. Becca looked just like Sheila, and she had the same gentle way about her. He didn't care what anyone said; she was his daughter. Their bond was a strong one.

Gail spread out a blanket, and then she set out food. A sweet picnic before the weather got colder. He smiled his thanks to Gail, and she blushed. He'd told her that there wasn't a future for them, but he had a feeling she didn't believe him.

It had been hard to watch Teagan, Quinn, and Brogan all adding to their families. Brogan now had twin girls. In fact, most of the babies had been female. His other brothers seemed content to be bachelors, but one never knew…

Hugs wouldn't be denied, and she tried to steal Becca's food. Becca laughed and scolded the dog and then laughed again. He ran his fingers through his hair. Days like this were when he longed for Sheila, for all the special moments they could have shared.

BECCA HAD GROWN and she was so beautiful and tall. She was happy, that much was obvious, and Sheila should have walked away, but she couldn't. She lay in the tall grass at the edge of the forest and watched. The new wife was very attractive, and she laughed often with Becca. That was a good thing. If only he'd told her in a letter instead of just deserting her. She understood that he needed a woman in his life, but she'd never understand the cowardly way he broke things off with her.

Sullivan... He was as handsome as ever. Her heart cried out to his, but it went unheard. It was fine. Really it was. It was for the best. They didn't have other children yet. It was probably her imagination, but Sullivan looked away from the woman more than he looked at her.

She was so tired. She'd gotten to where she wanted and seen Becca. It was time to go. What had happened to her property? Had they sold it? It would be too much to use up her energy getting to her old home only to find someone else living there. She lay there and watched her daughter and the man who held her heart, just resting. The longing to be part of such a picture grew immense.

Sullivan had done as she'd asked, and she'd have to be happy with that. She no longer belonged in their untainted lives. He was still a handsome man... with a few additional lines on his face. The only way she'd survived that vile place were dreams of Becca and him. They'd given her something to hold on to and it would have to be enough. It would just lead to upset and heartbreak if she revealed herself.

It seemed a long while before they packed up and went inside. When the door shut, it also shut on her dreams. But what was done was done. There wasn't a thing she could do about it. She crawled back into the forest and made her way to her cabin... if there was one. She'd not starve, she knew every plant she walked past. She'd need to get busy picking berries and the like but...

Her house was a beautiful two-story log structure. Tears filled her eyes. They had gone ahead on their plans despite her wanting to be the one who decided. A new barn and outhouse also sat on the property.

She made herself comfortable in the woods and ate the berries she had plucked from the bushes. Such a beautiful house must have someone living in it. Losing the house had pained her. She repeated the same Psalm she'd recited at least daily for the last three years. Psalm 23. *The Lord is my Shepherd...*

Sitting on land that once belonged to her, maybe it still did, was surreal. Someone had taken care of the grounds around the house. Flowers had been planted. The more she looked, the more convinced she was that someone else now owned her property.

Why hadn't Sullivan divorced her? He was an honorable man. He wouldn't be involved with that other woman if he didn't believe himself free, would he? Did he even think of her once in a while? No! She didn't make it through something so horrible only to be destroyed by thinking negatively.

She needed to count her blessings and seeing Becca safe and happy had been what she'd prayed for. God *was* listening. There were times she wanted to just fall and die where she lay, but she always felt a surge of strength and faith in those moments and she was able to continue on. In prison, those who fell were just shot. Most of the women had been disowned by their families. The guards didn't have to account for the prisoners lives at all.

She was getting cold. She got cold easier than before, and most times all she could do was shake. She waited for hours until the sun went down. She waited for the smallest flicker of light coming from inside the house, but there wasn't one.

HER BONES ACHED as she stood. She'd been sitting too long. Slowly, she approached the house and peered into all the windows on the first level. There were a few pieces of furniture. There was even a cook stove. She went around back and tried the door, but it was locked. It figured. She could burrow under the house into the root cellar, but she wouldn't be able to get into the house unless they'd cut a door in the floor.

Glass was too dear to break, but she was desperate. She took a big rock and threw it through a window in the back of the house. Three years ago, she would have been able to jump onto the windowsill and crawl inside. Now, she hunted for a rock large enough to give her a bit of a boost. Finally, she found one, rolled it in place with great effort, and finally struggled through the window and inside the house.

If anyone had been in the house, all the noise she'd made would have alerted them. Thank goodness for the light of the moon. She walked through the rooms, struck by one thing. No one had lived here. She went toward the front door, and on the wall hung a carved piece of wood with hooks at the bottom to hang keys. Someone had carved a name across it: Kelly. She'd never seen a better thing in her life. She traced the letters with her fingers. Sullivan must be saving the house for Becca.

She pulled a wooden chair from the kitchen to the front window. She wouldn't make a fire until she was sure no one was about. She watched for a long time. There were plenty of deer to be had, but that was all she saw. There was a bit of scrap wood piled next to the fireplace, but the stove would give off less light.

She made the fire and then put water on to boil. The water from the indoor water pump. What a gift! Someone had used the pump, for she didn't have to prime it. That meant someone had been inside the house. She'd have to be extra careful.

Wandering upstairs, she was amazed that there were three bedrooms, all with beds in them. One room contained a smaller bed that had heavy blankets on it. Glancing upward, she whispered, *Thank You*. The Lord had provided.

The blankets warmed her when she pulled them around her, and then she went back downstairs to the stove. She dragged the wooden chair in front of the stove, and then she grabbed a tin cup. It didn't matter, there was no food, just sipping on hot water would be a treat.

Once she was settled, she sipped many cups of hot water. The almost clear soup and tea they had fed her every day had always been cold in the winter and warm in the summer. She'd suggested planting a garden, and she'd been willing to do all the work in it. She had thought maybe they'd be happy to have something to put in the soup, but she just got a smack to the head for her suggestion. It had occurred to her that very likely they'd wanted the inmates to die of starvation.

This was the first time in over three years she'd felt safe. Eventually she laid on the floor wrapped in the blankets and slept.

CHAPTER ELEVEN

Sullivan was going crazy. He'd thought he saw Sheila in the woods a couple times. She'd looked very troubled and terribly thin, but when he'd look again, she'd be gone. She'd haunted his dreams and now she was haunting him during the day. But then again, he saw her every time he looked at Becca.

Gail had been with them about a year. At first, he was afraid one of his brothers would steal her away and marry her, but no one ever did. They'd all helped him with Becca for a long time until finally he realized he was keeping them from going on with their lives. Gail was nice and Becca had taken to her.

Often, he'd found Gail watching him, and that made him uncomfortable. He still loved Sheila. He'd tried and tried to forget about her, to move on from her, but he just couldn't. He did like Gail though, and they got on well. Maybe… seeing an apparition of Sheila… was a sign that he should move on. He'd told Gail there was no future for them, but maybe… they could be happy.

The sun beat down on him as he urged Zealous to move

forward, his decision made. Tonight, he'd ask her tonight before he changed his mind. Maybe that would chase Sheila's ghost away. It was for the best. Then he'd encourage Donnell to take the plunge. He was past the age to get married.

He had no ring for Gail. He had a ring he'd bought for Sheila, but he'd never part with it. The ranch had been making good money of late, though, and he could afford to buy another one for Gail. It was the logical next step, but it didn't feel entirely right. Maybe it never would. Maybe nothing would. He'd probably never find another who'd fit in with him and Becca again. He'd have to get a house built. Dolly would probably want them to live in Becca's house, but he just couldn't.

Later that night he asked Gail if she'd like to go for a walk. By the expressions on a few of his brother's faces, he would have thought he'd never walked with a woman before.

Once outside, he offered his arm and she took it. It was a nice, comfortable feeling, peaceful even. He gave her a side-long glance, and she looked confused. He stopped near the barn, turned, and took both of her hands in his. She was lovely with her brown curls and blue eyes.

"It's a nice night," he commented.

"Yes, it is." She studied him, and he felt awkward.

"Will you marry me?" he rushed out.

"Why? I mean this is very sudden." She stared into his eyes.

"I thought since we've known each other a while now and I admire you, marriage might be an agreeable thing. I never asked if you ever wanted children or not, but you seem to do well with Becca." He placed his hand on the side of her graceful neck. He didn't feel much when he touched her, but he was afraid it would be that way with all women. "We get on well, and you wouldn't have to worry about employment or anything. Besides, Becca is quite taken with you."

Her eyes clouded momentarily, and then she smiled. "Yes, Sullivan, I'll marry you."

He bent and kissed her lips. He felt guilty for a moment, but he shut those feelings out and deepened the kiss. He could only hold it for a moment. "Let's tell the rest."

"I think we should talk to Becca first. Her feelings need to be considered," Gail told him.

"You're not backing out, are you?" he asked with a quick grin.

"Of course not. This is unlike you to be impulsive. Did something happen to prompt the proposal?" She tilted her head, waiting for an answer.

"I've been thinking about it for a while now. We'll need to have a house built, and I thought we could pick the place together."

"You and Becca have a perfectly good house, all ready to move into. Now that you've accepted Sheila is dead, certainly you're ready to move on…" Her voice was gentle.

He jerked unintentionally. "I hadn't thought of it that way. We could go out there tomorrow and take a look before we talk to Becca. I want everything planned out before we approach her."

"I agree. We might need a long engagement. She still believes her mother is coming back to her. She prays for her every night."

He nodded. "I've heard her. This will help her in the long run. Death is so hard, especially a mother's death. So, I agree, we'll have a long engagement. We can get to know each other more. I don't know all that much about your background."

"Let's save that for another evening."

They walked into the house hand in hand, and Dolly subjected him to a hard stare. He quickly dropped Gail's hand. Dolly would ask him too many questions he wasn't yet ready to answer.

THE NEXT AFTERNOON, Sheila heard horses riding up to the house. She grabbed the blankets and ran upstairs and then farther up into the attic. They'd know someone had been in the house, but she hoped they would conclude that person was long gone.

The door below opened and closed. She hid behind a stack of planked wood. It was probably one of her brothers-in-law. Then she heard the laughter of a woman. Just what she needed, some harlot and her lover using this house as a love nest. She might be up here for a while.

She hadn't been feeling so great lately. She had overfed herself and ended up bringing most of it back up. She was even thinner than before. She'd known better too, but the temptation of food had been overwhelming. Little by little, her stomach stopped rebelling. She looked horrid, though. Her mother had once called her hair her crowning glory, but now it was dull and thin and almost the same color of the rats she had shared a cell with.

"How's my daughter?" a man asked.

Sheila shivered. That was not Sullivan's voice. *Able!* She had to cover her mouth from gasping.

"She is wonderful. I spend all day with her," answered a woman. "She's almost forgotten she had another mother," she added with confidence.

"Good, now what did you need to tell me?"

"Sullivan proposed to me last night. I played it off as it being too soon. He still misses the witch, but he said it's time to move on. He wants a long engagement, but I'll drag him to the altar sooner. Then I'll be Becca's mother, and a few months after the wedding Sullivan will have a deadly accident."

"Finally, I'll be the winner. I'll have the kid." He sounded to be bragging.

"You might have the kid, but I'll have the money."

"We're sharing the money, remember?" There was an underlining warning in his voice.

"Listen, don't get all cocky on me. I don't want any suspicions when he dies. Nothing comes back on me, you hear? I'm doing you a favor!"

"You'll just be the poor rich widow who leaves town with the money and the girl in tow."

"I just didn't want you to be surprised by the news and start blabbing. You've been staying away from the saloon, haven't you? This must remain between us and don't go getting impatient on me. It'll take as long as it takes," the woman said.

"It's been three years since they sent the witch to jail, and I still don't have Becca! The Kavanaghs have thwarted me at every turn," he roared.

"I've only been working on it for a little while."

"It's been what, a year or so? Your charms aren't delighting him. You must get him to compromise you. I told you that from the start."

There was a long pause. "Have you forgotten I'm not some floozy? Plus, he's too honorable to do anything like that. Look, I've finally got my proposal so stay out of it."

"Someone's been here in the house," Able said.

"That would be Sullivan. We're moving in as soon as we are married. He was most likely checking on the place."

Able was quiet. Then, "You're probably right. I will head out."

IT TOOK every fiber of her being not to scream. How dare they! How dare they try to steal her daughter? Her hands shook as she went over what she'd just heard. Sullivan was getting married? He still missed the witch? Her shoulders slumped. If he was ready to get married, he'd truly put her behind him. Would they remind Becca about her, or would Gail become the new mama while the real one was erased?

And why was Able still in town? She took a gulping breath. Sullivan had protected Becca all these years. But Becca was *her* daughter. She hung her head. A mother she'd be better off without, a mother to be ashamed of. Somehow, she'd have to warn Sullivan of the plot against him without allowing him to know she was in the area. His life was in danger, and how long would they keep Becca alive after they got the money they were after?

How she wished she could hold her little girl in her arms again. Just one more time. It was so hard to say goodbye, and Becca would never understand the reason she stayed away was for love. Once Gail and Able were out of Becca's life, then she'd leave the area. The gossip alone would ruin Becca's chance to make friends and eventually a good marriage. If they got a look at her in her condition... She shook her head. How she wished she could stay, but sometimes people had to let the ones they loved the most go.

She could talk to one of his brothers maybe, but Sullivan would want to know where the information came from, and he might come after her. She was too tired to run at the moment. So a long engagement would work to her benefit... as long as Gail didn't do something to move the date up. She didn't trust that woman.

The light outside was growing dim as dusk approached. She needed to check her traps and see if she'd caught any rabbits. Food and fur, both would be a Godsend.

Trying to ignore the tightening around her heart didn't

make the pain go away. She couldn't blame Sullivan one bit, but her heart didn't agree. It was time he moved on; it would be hard being married to a woman such as her, one convicted —albeit wrongly—of killing a child, one who had been sent to prison. The fact that it had taken him as long as it did surprised her, seeing as he never visited her or answered any of her letters. She'd been nothing but foolish thinking it had been a once in a lifetime love. The type of love that poets wrote about.

She took one of the blankets and wrapped it around her, then belted it like a coat. With that little protection, she went into the forest. She stopped at the stream that was nearby, and when she saw her reflection, she wept. Finding shelter had done nothing to help her physical condition. It was a wonder she'd been able to walk the whole way back home. She looked as though a fierce wind could knock her over.

She dried her eyes and went on to her traps. Three rabbits! A good haul. She'd smoke the meat of two of them and cook the third. She kept her eyes open and found wild onion. It would make a nice addition to the rabbit.

How long had it taken to build the house? It was beyond anything she would have thought of building herself. And one day it would be where Becca would live. As long as Sheila could stop the nefarious plans of Able and that woman. No, *when* she stopped them, she told herself sternly. *When*, not if. A few carpenter tools had been left in the barn. If the right tools were there, she'd carve something lovely on the mantel. Becca would have something from her after all.

As she approached the house, she stopped short and stared at the two horses tied outside. One was Zealous! Her heart raced. The other horse must be Gail's. She dropped back into the woods and waited. It drained the rest of her energy, sitting and waiting. The pain was too much to bear.

The Lord is my Shepherd...

She repeated it over and over, and then she walked away from the house. She couldn't bear it if Sullivan saw her again. Maybe she could get a note to him telling him about Gail. That she could do. She'd have to use charred wood as a pencil, but there were scraps of paper in the attic. Now, how to get it to him?

IT TOOK a while for her to decide what to write. If she wrote from her heart, he'd know she was out of jail. If it sounded like a rumor, he might just ignore it. After she wrote it that evening, she slipped through the woods and tied the note to the clothesline with a piece of twine. Dolly would see that it got to Sullivan.

She had to get back and sleep. Her strength needed replenishing. Prison had been a nightmare, especially the hard labor they'd been forced to perform. Of all the work in the world, it had been decided women needed to work in the rock quarry to be punished. It was beyond the bounds of humanity. At least she'd been young enough and strong enough to lift the rocks, but many of the women didn't even get that far. Sometimes when she closed her eyes, she'd still hear the screams of the women being beaten. Many of the prisoners were in there because of a man. But the tales were so outrageous, she'd become hard and jaded listening to them, only believing about half she heard. Some of those women were born evil.

Her lungs hurt trying to breathe in the cold air. She hadn't had time to gather her roots for medicine. She pulled the makeshift coat tighter around her. She'd be just fine in the morning.

SULLIVAN WATCHED Dolly's eyes grow wider and wider as she stared at a piece of paper in her hand.

"What's wrong?" he asked.

She shook her head. "I need to talk to you alone when you have a chance."

He smiled at Gail and Becca. "I have time now. Shall we go into Dad's office?"

She led the way, and he followed. What had her so upset? He closed the door behind them and was bowled over when Dolly poured two whiskeys. She downed hers and handed one to him. The note must be really bad.

"We should—"

"Read it." She shoved the paper into his hands.

DOLLY, I know you'll find this first, and I ask you kindly to pass it on to Sullivan. He needs to know about what I just found out. It's important, though it might be hurtful, but I can't spare him the hurt. The woman he has asked to marry him and Able Langton are working together. They talked about her wedding to Sullivan. Able wants Gail to be found in a compromising position to move the wedding up. The plan is to marry and then kill Sullivan, leaving Gail as Becca's guardian and a rich widow. The whole thing is about money. Becca can't fall into Able's hands. Please ask Sullivan to protect her. I know he thinks of her as his own. She needs him now more than ever.

IT WASN'T SIGNED. He read it three times and still couldn't figure out who might have sent it except for maybe the widow who had lived near Sheila and Becca years ago.

"I think a woman wrote it," Dolly said. "If I didn't know better, I'd think poor Sheila had written it."

His heart started beating double time. "But we do know

better," he said in a husky whisper. He sat down and swirled the amber drink around in the glass, watching it and thinking. "We shouldn't jump to conclusions. Gail has never given us reason to doubt her. She's been here over a year for crying out loud. Maybe this is from someone who wants to marry me. I mean, I can't think of anyone, but who knows? Maybe someone just doesn't want me to be happy. I'll have Donnell investigate it, he's good at that stuff. We need to act normal." He sighed. "I'm no good at acting normal."

"You'll have to do your best." Dolly put her hand on his shoulder. "We both will."

"I will protect my daughter with my life."

CHAPTER TWELVE

"*N*o one I talked to knew much about her background except that she's from St. Louis," Donnell said a little more than a week later as he and Sullivan sat in the office before a flickering fire. "You say she claims to be a widow, but according to my sources in Missouri she was never married. She uses her mother's last name. I'm working on finding her father's name. I believe her parents are dead, but there's nothing nefarious about her except for not using her real last name." Donnell crossed his feet at the ankles and relaxed. "She's a decent young lady who works as a nanny." He took a sip of his coffee and then he frowned. He put his finger to his nose and nodded toward the closed door.

A shadow of someone standing outside the door was apparent, and Sullivan's gut clenched. He started to stand, but Donnell shook his head and gestured for Sullivan to sit back down.

"I'm sorry I investigated your bride-to-be, but I wanted to look out for you," Donnell said in a loud voice.

"I know all I need to know, and no I'm not mad. Perhaps

before the war I might have slugged you, but we need to have each other's backs. I'm thinking about talking to Gail and setting a date. I want many more children. Hopefully boys to run the ranch." After a brief pause, he added, "I just wished I'd saved my money." Then he winked at Donnell. "I can't afford much of a house, but I can fix up one of the line shacks and we'll live on love for a while."

"What about Becca's house?"

"Too many memories. I've left those all behind." Sullivan fell silent after that. His throat burned as he said those last words. He so loved his wife, but he had never had a chance to show her. He longed to remember her touch, but they'd touched so few times, it was hard to remember anything.

The shadow disappeared.

Sullivan sat forward. "Who do you think it was? I can't imagine anyone of our family would listen in on a conversation."

"I'm sorry, but I think it might have been Gail," Donnell said.

Sullivan nodded and slumped back into his chair. "What is going on? I swear I'm going mad. My mind even has me seeing Sheila in the woods at times."

"You mean when you're sleeping?"

"No, not a dream. It's more like a ghost, but I always thought ghosts were floating or something. She looked awful, so worn and so thin, like she'd been sick for a long time. Maybe she was sick for a while before she died. They'd refused to answer any of my questions." He felt as though the entire world was sitting on his shoulders and he was about to be crushed.

"We still don't know who wrote the note," Donnell whispered. "I keep thinking of the possibilities, and I come up blank."

"Same here. It'll be another sleepless night for me."

"I'm sorry, Sullivan. If there is anything I can do, just ask."

"I appreciate it. I'm going to tuck Becca in. Good night."

He heard Donnell say good night as he walked out of the office. He should just escort Gail off the property, but in the long run that wouldn't protect Becca. It might be best if he took Becca to another part of Texas and started over. He just didn't know what to do. Nothing had been right since Sheila had been arrested. Nothing would ever be right again.

As far as he was concerned, Becca was his daughter. Their shared grief had made their bond very tight. He loved her so. Why would Able do this now? He'd made a couple of half-hearted attempts to take Becca when Sheila had first been taken away, but he'd given up early on. He must have met Gail and talked her into his scheme. Gail must have come to the ranch to be close to Becca. But why wait a year? Things did not add up, but he would get to the bottom of it for both Becca and Sheila's sake.

THE NEXT MORNING Sullivan rode to Widow Muse's home. The place was overgrown. He hadn't given the woman a second thought since he'd collected Becca from her when Sheila had first been on the run, but perhaps he should have. Sheila would have expected him to look in on her.

He knocked, and a burly man answered the door. "Whatcha want?"

"I was hoping to see Widow Muse. Does she still live here?

The man turned and yelled over his shoulder, "Ma! There's someone here to see you. Want me to send him on his way?"

"For heaven's sake Lawrie, who is it?" A spry Mrs. Muse came to the door. A grin spread over her face. "I remember you. You're Sullivan, aren't you?"

"Yes, ma'am. I was wondering if I could talk to you about Becca."

She pushed her son aside and gestured for Sullivan to come on in. "I have some tea made. Come and have a cup with me. I love that little one and I have missed her dearly. That no good Able came here after the sentencing looking for Becca. I didn't contact you; I thought it to be better if I stayed away." She hurried ahead of him and offered him a seat at the table. She quickly had a cup of tea before him.

Sullivan came right to the point. "Mrs. Muse… Someone left me a note telling me that Gail and Able planned to take Becca once Gail and I married."

She nodded slowly. "Yes… Able has been lying low with plenty of time for his hate to fester. He can be a real sweet talker, and he probably persuaded that poor woman Gail to help him. Sullivan, you can't be married to two people at the same time. You do know that, right?"

He almost choked on his tea. "What are you talking about? I'm a widower. I have been for a long while now."

The widow frowned. "No, Sullivan, she's not dead. I've received a letter or two from her. The last one said she was getting out soon. That one came maybe four months ago." She tilted her head and appeared to be considering something. "Or was it six? She should be getting out now or maybe she's already out."

His jaw dropped as anger filled him. "At first no one would tell me where she was. I sent telegrams to the judge demanding to see her but was told I had to wait three months. Once I found out her location, I went there immediately, and I was told by the warden she was dead. I wasn't even allowed to see her grave. It tore at me, not being able to be at her graveside to say goodbye. They never notified me of her death. Becca refused to leave my side for the first two years and finally I hired Gail when she came to the ranch looking for a job."

"Oh my! I wish I had known. I could have saved you from grieving. Oh, my poor Becca. If I see anything out of the ordinary, I'll let you know."

"I seen that Able meet with your woman Gail at the house near here. It's an eerie place. I went there once and heard noises, but I never found anyone," Lawrie said. "I'll keep an eye out too. I just moved back here. The army was my life and most recently the Cavalry, but I didn't have the stomach for hunting down Indians."

"Your mother has great grazing land. If you ever need a few heads of cattle to start a herd, stop on by the ranch. I'm going to Becca's house to check things out. I can hardly believe my wife was alive—I mean *is* alive." He stood and touched the tip of his hat before he left.

He quickly jumped up on Zealous and rode toward the house they'd built for Sheila and him. He'd taken Gail there recently. It hurt too much to be there. He stared at the house for a while. How could she be alive, and he not know it? His stomach clenched and he felt heartsick. Over three years and he had never gotten a letter from her. It hurt. Sighing, he tipped his hat back. Catching sight of what he thought could be a shadow moving by the upstairs window, he stiffened. He might as well check it out.

The leather of his saddle creaked as he slid off his horse. The widow must be mistaken. She was getting on in years, maybe her mind had begun to go feeble. He opened the door and walked inside. Just as he'd expected, it was empty and silent. He had tried not to get his hopes up, but his eyes glistened. It didn't much matter what the widow said or thought she knew. Sheila was dead. There was no way Sheila would be alive and not be with Becca. He hated this house. He'd love to just set a match to the place, but it didn't belong to him. It was Becca's.

It was much bigger than the house Sheila had before. She would have had much more room to dry her plants. But her talent had gotten her killed and for naught. After they took her away, people started coming forward in her defense. Where had they been when they were needed? No one had stood up for her. For a long time, he refused to go to church until Gemma reminded him that the church didn't belong to other people, it belonged to God, and she was sure he was invited to be there. He went, ignoring the people gawking at him, and he prayed. The third time he attended, he had finally felt God in his heart, and it had amazed him.

The house sounded empty; he'd forgotten to tell Donnell about the broken window. It still needed to be repaired. He might as well check the upstairs. The steps creaked near the bottom. Then he heard something moving above him and he took off at a run. He ran to where he thought the noise came from, but no one was there. He noticed the door to the attic was open.

SHEILA STAYED AS quiet as possible. She covered her mouth as her heart pounded. It sounded so loud to her. Could he hear it? He was right next to where she was hidden. Turning her head, she looked up and saw his astonished expression as he met her gaze.

She slowly and painfully stood, her body shaking. Did he recognize the old hag before him? She still didn't fill out her dress properly and her pitiful hair…

"Sheila?" He stood there staring.

"Yes, I—I know I look different." She shook uncontrollably. "The last three years and then the last month took a toll. Well, surviving was the hardest thing I've ever done. Few women ever leave prison." What more was there to say? He had never visited or sent a letter. She'd written him often, but she had never heard back. He'd abandoned her. It happened to every prisoner eventually she had discovered, so although it tore her heart out, she hadn't been surprised.

He jumped over the stacked lumber and put his hands on her shoulders, looking her up and down. He must pity her. Tears sparkled in his eyes.

Sheila shrugged out of his hands and took a step back. "Hello, husband… or did you have the marriage annulled?"

His brow furrowed. "Annulled? No, of course not."

Looking at his handsome face so close to her was harder than she thought it would be. "I'm leaving. Don't follow me." Turning, she slowly made her way down one set of stairs and then another. She took her blankets and held them tight, and then she walked out the door and into the woods.

Sullivan made no attempt to follow.

He must think her stupid. A man didn't marry a woman when he already had a wife. It wasn't legal. He probably didn't need an annulment. He could just tear up the papers. They never consummated the wedding.

She shuffled on through the woods until she came to a tree that was empty inside, at least at the bottom up to just past her head. Anyone walking by would never notice it if they weren't looking for it. Once inside, she drew the blankets around her and sat.

He'd looked surprised to see her. She'd thought release notices were supposed to be sent to the prisoner's family. No matter. She drew the blanket closer around her. It was getting damp inside the tree, and her body wouldn't stop shivering. To take her mind off the cold, she gave some consideration to her circumstances. The only thing she owned was the house and the supplies and money she had buried long ago. If they were still there. She'd be a fool to leave the house in her condition. Perhaps if she changed her name, her presence wouldn't affect Becca.

It buoyed her spirits a bit. She climbed out of the tree and walked back to the house. It might be interesting to have a new identity. She'd make one up in case it was needed. A name, something that would blend in. Marta Bauer would fit. There were a few German settlements around, and Bauer seemed to be a popular name. *Marta Bauer.* It was a pretty name. Of course she'd never fool most, but if she went back to her hermit style of living, she should be fine.

CHAPTER THIRTEEN

*S*heila turned in a circle, admiring her house. It looked good. She hadn't been able to buy much, but she had the basics. Lawrie Muse had been a big help; going to town and then delivering the items to her.

It had been a week since she'd stood in front of Sullivan. He'd ridden out each day, but she'd barred the door and hidden upstairs. There was no reason to talk to him. She jutted her chin. She could perfectly run her own life. Then her shoulders sagged. What she wouldn't give to hold Becca again, though. Her eyes grew moist. She wasn't being heroic or strong; she was just a coward. Hearing why he didn't even care enough to answer her letters would be the death of her. But she had a burning inside of her that had to know the reason.

She ran her hands down the calico dress she'd sewn. Her world had changed once more when she took off her threadbare gray shift that was her prison uniform. She'd even tried a few hairstyles that didn't make her look like a beggar.

While in prison, she had craved solitude, now she hated

the loneliness that came with it. She was supposed to have thought about her crime and repented while in prison. Shaking her head, she frowned. She'd had nothing to repent.

She'd foraged in the forest every day. It made her feel free. She put on her new cape and grabbed a basket. She had a poke bonnet to put on, but she liked the feel of the wind through her hair. After checking her rifle, she set out.

The first thing she gathered was willow bark. It helped keep her bones from hurting so much. Next, she looked for sage. A twig snapped, and she whirled around, ready to fight, releasing a sigh when she recognized Sullivan. "Just leave me alone." She returned to her pursuit of sage.

Saying nothing, he stood right behind her, so close she felt the heat from his body.

"Is Becca sick?" She bent to gather the herbs.

"She's in fine health. Her heart can't seem to heal though."

"Doesn't she like the new mother you picked out for her?" Her voice was tart, but she didn't care.

"Are you trying to punish me? I haven't slept in nearly a week."

"That's not possible, and no I'm just giving as good as I got." She swallowed hard. The lump in her throat didn't disappear.

He sighed. "I don't understand what you mean. Please, Sheila, talk to me. Look at me."

She couldn't help herself; she turned. "It was much worse than you'd imagine the opposite of heaven to be."

"Hell."

"Yes," she whispered. "I waited and waited for any news of you and Becca. You would have thought a wise woman would have given up after a few months, but I'm not wise. I waited for three years and you answered not one of my letters. I did get one short note from the widow Muse but her mind rambles and so did her letter. It didn't matter, I read that note every night for months. It was all I had ever got, though I wrote many, hoping—" Quickly she glanced away. She needed to stay strong.

"The warden told me you were dead," he said, his voice getting harsher with each word.

"That's convenient. Other women got letters. No one said they were dead. Well, not until they actually died that is. Listen, I don't want Becca to know I'm here. I'd only be an embarrassment to her. She'll be teased and turned away for the rest of her life, and I refuse to allow that to happen. But you have to keep her safe!" she stressed. "And that means you cannot marry that girl. Gail, is it? I'm sorry if you love—Gail, but her plans to take Becca are not acceptable. Do what you want with her, but please keep her away from Becca. I heard her and Able talking and the plan is for you to be found in a compromising position with Gail. You'll be forced to marry." She turned her head again and met his gaze. "Please do this one thing for me... or rather do it for Becca. I'm afraid for her. Able must not get his hands on her."

Sullivan nodded. He opened his mouth to say something, but no words came out. Finally, he nodded again and left.

Watching him leave almost broke her—almost.

———

SULLIVAN FELT LOST. If he went into the house, Dolly would be sure to notice something was wrong and ask him all kinds of things. He wasn't up to it. He wasn't up for the laughter he heard from the barn. He was more up for punching something. But although that sounded good, it never helped.

Donnell came hurrying over. "I need to talk to you." He walked toward the stream, stopping where a small inlet formed a calm pool of water. "I don't want anyone to overhear us."

"What is it?"

"Remember when you got a wire that Sheila was dead? It wasn't true."

He angled his head and shot his brother a sarcastic stare. "Go on."

Donnell faltered. "You already knew?"

"Just very recently, but I don't understand any of it."

Donnell picked up a flat rock and skipped it across the stream. "Mr. Wren paid the sheriff and the judge to convict Sheila and then once she was in prison, more of Wren's money went to the warden."

Sullivan stumbled back as though he'd been sucker punched. "What? Why?" His heart sped up, and he couldn't make any sense of what Donnell was saying.

"I dug deeper into Sheila's case. We knew it was a crazy verdict, and I was suspicious. All those people who came forward at the end of the trial saying the little girl had been burned and was dead before they got to Sheila's… It took a while, but I got Mr. George the banker to trust me. That man is suspicious of everything. Took me a few years to get on his good side. Old Jim George finally gave up the fact that Wren withdrew money to pay off Sheriff Ganes and Judge Harvey. Then he told me about the payoff to Warden Stang. Ed Wren had something against Sheila. Everyone knows his girl was dead before she got to Sheila's house, but no one said anything until that lawyer you got her pressed them under oath. Her own mother kept saying she was burned and already dead when her pa took her. Even then, the judge declared her guilty. I can't make heads nor tail of it."

Sullivan's face heated. "Where is Wren now? I heard he moved." He kept his voice stone cold but even.

"I'm looking. Don't do anything that will put you behind bars. Nothing you can do to Sheriff Ganes since he was shot dead a while ago. And you know that judge hasn't been back."

He settled a hand on Sullivan's shoulder and squeezed. "I'm taking a ride out to the prison to see what I can find on the warden."

"She thought I didn't bother to write to her or visit her. Sheila thought I annulled our marriage. Right now, she thinks Becca is better off if she continues to stay away."

"You'll have to convince her otherwise." Donnell patted Sullivan's shoulder once, then dropped his arm and walked away.

Sullivan picked up a couple of stones and flicked them outward, watching them skip across the water. He needed to do two things. Stay away from Gail, never be alone with her, and win Sheila back. Actually, he had a third thing; keep a close eye on Becca.

He closed his eyes, trying to remember all Sheila had said. She spent over three years hurting and hating him, thinking he had abandoned her. He had mountains to climb to get her back. She looked so fragile, but she was still tough. She was a proud woman, an independent woman, a stubborn woman. And she was his woman. She was alive! It should have been a time of celebration, but that wouldn't happen if he couldn't get his wife to trust him. If he'd had his way, he would have brought her home with him. Now *that* would have been a fight. He was out of his element. He needed Dolly.

It wasn't until after supper that he was able to get her alone. He looked around the first floor and didn't see anyone. He didn't want to be overheard, but there were too many places to hide and listen inside the house. Better yet, he got his coat and Dolly's wrap.

She gave him an inquiring look.

"I need to talk to you alone."

With no hesitation, she put on her wrap and followed him outside.

"I know it's cold, but someone was listening in when I was talking to Donnell in the office a few weeks back."

"I'm fine. What's on our mind?"

"Sheila is alive."

It took Dolly a few seconds before her eyes widened. "What? Where is she?"

"She's at her house. And she thought I didn't bother to write to her or even visit. I need to talk to her for a length of time. Usually she has the door barred, and the two times I talked to her were short. She's afraid for Becca. She overheard Gail and Able plotting to get Becca. I believe she's the one who left that note. She doesn't believe anything I say and is positive I had our marriage annulled. I don't think she understands we thought her to be dead. She called it a convenient excuse."

"She believes that Becca forgot about her too?"

"A few letters got through from Widow Muse. That's proof enough for her we didn't write to her." Emotion welled, threatening to choke him. "Dolly, she looks half starved. Her eyes are sunken, and you can see her bones. Her hair is different, not lush, and shiny as it was. The first time I saw her she had on an ugly gray prison dress. It was very loose on her. But today she had on a calico dress and there isn't much of her left."

"Can you do without me tonight and for breakfast?"

He furrowed his brow. "I... why?"

"I'm going to talk to that wife of yours. I'll tell her how it was."

"It's too dark for you to travel."

Dolly laughed. "Too bad you didn't know me in my younger days." She turned and hurried into the house.

He shook his head. He'd get someone to follow to be sure Dolly arrived safely. He couldn't do it, couldn't leave Becca alone with Gail. He rubbed the back of his neck. How was he supposed to act like nothing was going on? He'd have to confide in Teagan and Gemma. They'd help.

After he hurried to the bunkhouse and talked Rafferty into following Dolly, he asked everyone to be extra watchful. Then he went into the main house.

"Daddy!" Becca jumped up, so he'd catch her. And she gave him a bright, loving smile. "Will you tell me a bedtime story and hear my prayers?"

"Sure!" He looked up and his eyes met Gail's. "I think Gail could use a little time to herself."

"I will heat more water. I'm taking a bath. Don't worry, I'll remember to put the privacy screens in place and lock the back door this time." She chuckled.

Sullivan made himself smile at her. "It's the back door that gets us all at least once." He carried Becca up to her room.

THE KNOCK on Sheila's door was very light. She grabbed her rifle anyway and opened the door. It was like coming home, seeing Dolly on her porch. Her heart wanted to sing. "Come in. Are you alone? It's too dark out to travel alone."

Dolly entered the house. "Rafferty trailed me the whole way. That boy was never quiet from the first." She held up a small bag. "I'm here to spend the night with you. It's the only time I have to myself and I wanted to spend it with you." She put her bag down and took off her wrap. After she put her hands on her hips, she shook her head. "They only fed you enough to stay alive, didn't they?" Dolly then wrapped Sheila into her embrace and held her tight.

Finally, Sheila could cry for all that she'd lost. She wept for all the injustice, the pain, the heartbreak and lies. She wept for her worry for Becca, and she wept for her loss of herself. She didn't know who she was or how she fit in.

When the worst was over, Dolly made a big fire and set two chairs in front of it. She gently settled Sheila into one of them. "I'll put up the water for tea."

At least if Sheila died, Dolly knew what was in her heart to tell Becca. She was embarrassed to be a shell of the woman she was.

"Here we go. This will warm you up." Dolly handed her a cup of tea and then moved a small table next to Sheila's chair. "I made cookies and figured you'd like a few." Then she sat in the other chair.

"Thank you. No matter what I do, I never seem to be able to get warm. I've been chilled to the bone for a very long time. The cookies are much appreciated. I've been busy looking for plants for medicine and have had little time to spend in the kitchen."

"I'm so happy to see you," Dolly said, the firelight catching the glint of tears in her eyes. "I've missed you and there was a hole in my heart every time I looked at Becca. At first, she refused to believe you were dead. She'd cry herself to sleep every night. Sullivan then stayed in her room until she fell asleep. He didn't even leave on the cattle drives the last few years. He kept her with him at all times. Finally, she—I think she felt safe. This last year he hired Gail and was able to ride alone. He always loved being a cowboy." Heaving a sigh, she shook her head. "We all thought Gail was an honest and kind woman. But enough about her. Right after they took you away, Sullivan tried to find you and he finally found out and went to see you, but they insisted you were dead even though they wouldn't allow him to pay his respects at your grave. That man grieved for you something awful. He tried to be cheerful for Becca, and I do believe she kept him sane."

Sheila could only stare. Why on earth had someone told him she was dead?

Dolly took a sip of her tea. "My dear, you were never forgotten, not for a single moment. We all mourned for you, Becca, and Sullivan. Nothing was the same. Everything happened so fast we didn't have time to draw a breath. They whisked you away without allowing for goodbyes. Then no one would tell Sullivan where you were. He thought he failed you, but he was determined to keep his promise about Becca. Able made a fuss at first, but he didn't have the means to go up against the Kavanaghs. Deputy Moore became Sheriff, and he wanted no part of Able's scheme to get Becca. As to why Sullivan asked Gail to marry him, well, you know the brothers. They kept at him this last year, telling him he should remarry. He didn't have the heart to look at another woman, but Gail was there. There was nothing between them and even though they became engaged, I don't think there is anything between them still. Sullivan doesn't light up when he sees her like he did when he saw you."

"I thought he'd decided he didn't want me for his wife. I figured he loved Gail and they planned to make Becca theirs," Sheila explained. "I was the one who left the note on the clothesline."

"I realize that now," Dolly murmured.

"You can see why I didn't want anyone to see me," Sheila continued, gesturing to her body. "Most of the women in the prison died well before their release date. We were beaten and starved and worked to death. It was my need to see Becca again that kept me going. At night I'd think of Sullivan and Becca and what a happy family we'd be. As time went on Sullivan even left my dreams. I watched other women read their mail and it tore my heart anew each time. I was innocent. I couldn't understand why the judge couldn't see that. It made me a bitter person, and my vow to get even also kept me going."

"It was all done for money," Dolly said, shaking her head. "I believe Mr. Wren didn't want to admit he was wrong. He must have known his daughter was already dead. But he paid off the judge and the sheriff. No one has seen the judge in about a year, and the sheriff was shot about the same time. I suppose it was right before Gail showed up."

Sheila sighed. "How can anyone play with people's lives like that? I'm sure he'll get his due by the hand of God. I've decided to stay dead and live here as Marta Bauer. I don't want to ruin Becca's life. Having a convict for a mother, especially one who looks like I do now, will ruin any chance she'll have for happiness. Sullivan deserves better, too. I don't even recognize myself in the mirror. But I'll only be happy once Gail and Able are run off."

"You're not coming home?" Shock colored Dolly's words. "I think you should reconsider. Becca needs you, and Sullivan loves you. You look as skinny as all get out, but other than that, I'd know you anywhere. It's not what's on the outside, Sheila, it's what's in the inside that counts. Surely as a mother you can understand that."

Sheila was silent for a bit, considering Dolly's words. Then she nodded. "You're right. I'm going home with you in the morning. I thought I was making a sacrifice for my daughter, but it's me being selfish and afraid. I kept thinking, 'What if she runs from me?'"

"You never know how children will react, but I know you are in her heart," Dolly promised.

Sheila nodded. "I just wish there was someone who could clear my name. I guess there's no one else. It would have to be Ed Wren."

"And he's disappeared. But Donnell is looking for him. Donnell has turned out to be quite the investigator. He's been a rock for Sullivan. I know you and Sullivan would knock heads both wanting to be right. Sullivan is still bossy, but he no longer has to be right. He liked to be in control, but he's learned that he can't be in control. Life is about God's will. I see your gumption in your eyes, and I think you now know that everything isn't a battle. Let me help you into bed and in the morning, we'll pack up your things and go home."

Sheila had tears in her eyes as she hugged Dolly good night.

CHAPTER FOURTEEN

Sullivan played tag with Becca while he anxiously waited for Dolly to return. His heart pounded, wondering what Sheila would have told her. Had he lost his wife for good? It had ruined his life when he'd heard about her death, but now to know that she thought he hadn't wanted to write to her. How she must have suffered with those thoughts going through her mind. She had believed herself to be all alone. He turned and saw two women riding toward him on Dolly's horse. His hopes rose and his heart felt ready to explode.

He hurried toward the barn with Becca running to keep up with him. Once the paint stopped Sullivan lifted his arms and helped his love down and then held her so very close to him. He didn't want to let go. Finally, though, he set her on her feet, and Becca's eyes widened. She ran to her mother, almost knocking her over.

"Mama? Is it really you?"

Sheila kneeled in the dirt and hugged Becca with a look of joy on her face. The love in her eyes was there for all to see.

"Daddy, Mama is home!" Becca scrambled to him.

With wet eyes, he nodded. "It's a miraculous day." He helped Sheila up and kissed her forehead. "Welcome home."

"I thought you were in heaven, Mama..." Becca's bottom lip trembled. "Did you meet Jesus?"

"I prayed to him all the time, and now I'm here with you. There were a few times I thought I was going to heaven, but it wasn't my time, and thinking about you strengthened me. You kept me going, and now I'm here with you."

Sheila took a step and stumbled a bit. Sullivan instantly lifted her into his arms and smiled at her when she wrapped her arms around his neck. She was light as a feather, and that was the truth. She weighed barely more than Becca.

She smiled back.

"Our room? Becca's room? Or the sofa?" he asked as he climbed the steps to the porch.

"Sofa will be fine. I'm sure everyone will want to get a look at me."

He grimaced. There wasn't much to see. A frail, too-skinny woman. The love of his life.

"Of course, our family will want to welcome you home." He set her on the sofa, and Becca sat by her side. It was as it should be, but he didn't believe it would be easy.

Gail walked in and halted. "I didn't know we had guests." She cocked her brow at him. And that didn't sit well with him. Her tone was haughty.

"This is my wife, Sheila. It's a miracle she's alive, and we're filled with happiness that she has returned," Sullivan said as he gave Gail a hard stare.

Gail put a hand to her mouth. "I had no idea. Of course, this breaks our engagement. I'm sorry, I'm... it's a shock. This changes so much. I'm sorry; this isn't about my broken heart, it's about celebrating your return." Tears streamed down her face.

He wished he cared enough to say something comforting to her.

"Many things have changed," Sheila said. "There were too many underhanded misunderstandings. I'm still trying to figure out how people could lie the way they did, and yet even when some told the truth the judge still put me in prison. The lies piled up after that, too. So many people were hurt by the deceptions. I know you and my husband were engaged, and I know you must be… heartbroken. I can't say that I'm sorry to be back though."

"What if there's a child?" Gail turned to Sullivan.

Shock went from his head to his toes. "Excuse me?"

"I'm so embarrassed. What you must think of me." Gail went to the window and gazed outside.

Teagan and Gemma entered the room and instantly flanked Sullivan.

"The engagement was to be a long one. Why say you're with child now?" Gemma asked.

Gail turned around and frowned. "What are you saying, Gemma? You know you show the world how perfect you are, but I've seen you weeping a time or two lately. Your husband and girl are too much for you. Teagan deserves better."

Teagan took a step forward. "Gail that is enough. I'll have Angus go to town and see about getting you a job. You should pack now."

Gail's stare touched each of them before she walked to her room.

Gemma ran to the sofa and hugged Sheila. "What a happy surprise! I'm so very glad you're here. Now we can all have a piece of our hearts restored."

"Tell me, what did you name your child?" Sheila asked.

Gemma's expression was one of love. "Lacey. She looks just like Teagan."

"I have so much catching up to do. For now, I want to

spend time getting to know Becca and Sullivan again." Her voice was weary.

"I think a nap is in order," Sullivan said.

"I don't take naps, Daddy."

He chuckled. "I meant your mother. You can come if you like. I'm thinking about a nap too."

"That sounds like fun!" Becca ran upstairs ahead of them.

Sullivan leaned down, kissed Sheila's cheek, and then lifted her close to him. "I don't know how long—"

"I'll make sure no one disturbs you," Dolly said. Sullivan hadn't seen her this happy in a while.

Becca decided whose bed they would nap in, and she chose Sullivan's. Not that he minded one bit. He laid Sheila down, and she spooned with Becca. Then he got onto the bed and he spooned her from behind, able to put his arms around both of the females he loved. Sheila groaned as everyone shifted to get comfortable. Her thinness broke his heart. Had he known, he would have petitioned to get her released early. He should have done better by her.

───────

SHE WOKE and was tempted to scream, not that anyone took any notice of screams. Where was she? Then it came to her that she was safe in Sullivan's arms and Becca was with her. She never thought it would happen. Love pushed out much of her anger. Staying still, she enjoyed the warm feeling of sleeping next to Sullivan. It was the first time she hadn't been chilled to the bone in three years.

Becca had grown so very much. What a beautiful young girl she'd become. Pride filled Sheila. Becca attended school, and she had friends on the ranch. Well, actually the people on the ranch were family. It would take some doing, getting used to others helping her. She hoped Angus found Gail a job, not that it would stop Able, but she had already decided in prison she would tell the world about how he'd attacked her. His threats against her didn't matter any longer. He'd run before wanting everyone to know what had really happened between them. Becca was some sort of prize for him to win, but no longer. Her inner strength surprised and delighted her. There were bound to be too many changes on the ranch for her not to get overwhelmed. She needed to concentrate on Becca and Sullivan.

CHAPTER FIFTEEN

It was two weeks later, and Sheila felt very close to her daughter, but it was still painfully awkward with her husband. Slowly, she was getting to know the whole family again. They all tried to feed her at every turn, and they meant well, but she only could eat so much. She didn't know where Gail was working, and she didn't ask. She waited anxiously each day for Able to show up.

Living in fear took a lot of energy. There were times she wished she could just get a shotgun and hunt him down. She was tense all the time. It was hard to allow Becca out of her sight.

Finally, one sunny afternoon Dolly convinced her to go on a picnic with her husband. As much as her thoughts were often of him, she felt awkward around him. They slept in the same bed, but she clung to her side. There wasn't a reason for her to be afraid, but she was.

Sullivan took the basket in one hand and held her hand in his other. They were going near the stream. That way, Sheila could still run to the house if trouble came. Sullivan gave her hand a quick squeeze.

"I'm glad we will have time together alone. Don't worry, you don't even have to talk if you don't want to. I just want to gaze at you without everyone around. I want to figure out how to make you comfortable with me again. I know I let you down and I failed to protect you and I stupidly believed you were dead. I want you to trust me."

He stopped and put the basket down. Then he took the blanket from the top and shook it out flat for them to sit on. "I still can't believe you're here. Sometimes I wake in a panic that you being here, is a dream. I know you're still afraid that Able will come and take Becca, and I share in your fear, but he can't get to you or Becca. His lechery goes beyond any I've known. Trying to have Gail wed me to steal our daughter…" He shook his head. "I too have learned that trusting too easily can lead to disaster. I never felt toward her like I should and I never should have proposed to her."

"Yet you did," Sheila whispered as emotional pain speared through her.

He stared at the ground. "I knew I'd never have a love like I had for you ever again. I didn't want the pain of looking for a wife, and for some reason I felt that marrying again was expected of me. I thought Becca needed a woman in her life, but she already has the most amazing women in her life in Dolly and all her aunts. I buried any love I had when I thought they buried you. We never did have enough time to be together. We married one day, and they took you away the next." A shudder rippled through him, and he swallowed hard. "I had nightmares of you dying in that place. I tried to visit, and I heard the screams of women and I saw many laboring in the quarry and although it near killed me, I told myself I was glad at least you weren't experiencing what those women were."

"You wouldn't have thought there'd be so many women in prison," she said softly. "I know I was surprised. At first, I made a few friends, but they all kept dying. My heart needed to be protected, so I didn't make friends anymore. I kept my own council. I rarely talked. I just did what was needed to live through the day. The last year was the hardest. I reconciled myself with the fact you no longer wanted me. I felt utterly hopeless, but God was there. Who would have thought He'd be in such an awful place? But I held His hand many times. During beatings He was there, when it was almost too cold to move, He was there. When I was in despair, He was there. Even while we starved, I could feel the Lord with me. I do believe a few thought of me as touched in the head. I recited Psalm 23. I chanted it over and over, and it brought me a measure of peace. I do know without my faith, I'd be dead. It was much easier to lie down and die than it was to survive."

She sighed and then took a bite of her sandwich. "I too feel guilty for not trusting you. I should have known you wouldn't have left me. I'm very sorry."

"You don't need to be sorry." He touched her hand. "We were both deceived. I also found God while you were gone. I would have gone crazy if not for my ability to pray. And now we have a second chance. We should throw away the deceit and rejoice about the miracle that we are a family again. I have too many blessings to count. Will you come to church with me on Sunday?" He popped a berry into his mouth.

With one hand, she waved half-heartedly at her body. "I look pitiful."

Sullivan reached up and caressed her cheek. "You are so beautiful to me. You just remember your soul might have been bruised, but it was never broken. You stood strong. Few people can say they've done the same."

Hope washed over her, along with pride. "I will go with you."

He took her hand and kissed her knuckles. "Now for the

awkwardness we've been feeling. I know we never consummated our marriage. I won't push you, but I want to at least hold you at night. I need to know you are safe and with me. The rest will come in time."

Her face heated, and she couldn't bring herself to look at him. "I thought with all my bones jutting out it would be hurtful for you to hold me. You don't know what it means to me that you are taking my feelings into consideration. I lived like an animal, and the niceties and attention you have shown me touch me deeply. I feel as though I've taken so much for granted, but I feel blessed to realize what I have in you and Becca. Your family is wonderful, too. I would like to live in our own house, eventually. I don't know that I'm ready yet. I'm still on edge about Able and Gail. Plus, the Wrens were out to get me, and I don't know why. Even though they seem to have left the area, I think staying at the ranch house for now is the best. You can better protect us there."

His smile blossomed in her heart. God was truly with her. How could a person feel such love? It was almost too much.

"I don't know that I've enjoyed a time better than this," Sullivan said as he stood.

Sheila packed up the last of the items and folded the blanket. She tripped over a corner and Sullivan steadied her. They gazed at each other and the next thing she knew she was being kissed with such sweetness it almost made her cry. Blessed, she was indeed blessed.

THEY WALKED hand in hand back to the house. Sullivan felt better about their relationship than he had since Sheila's return. He helped her up into bed. She'd been taking a nap each afternoon; she was still very weak, but she'd been eating and helping around the house a bit. Becca, who until this point had sworn off naps, now snuggled with her mama each day.

He tucked them in and kissed them each on the forehead before heading back down the stairs. Sheila would never feel safe unless Able was gone. He needed to see what he could do about that.

Hoofbeats sounded from outside, and he peeked through a window to see Teagan and Quinn just riding in. As soon as they were off their horses, they walked straight to the house.

"We found some interesting information in town today, well actually Donnell did," Teagan said as he hung up his hat and then sat down. "There's a wanted poster for Gail. Sheriff Moore showed it to us. Apparently, she stole a lot of valuable jewelry from her previous employer,"

"And we were able to track her family. She and Ed Wren are brother and sister," Quinn added.

"How does that even play out? I can't even think of a scenario that fits," Sullivan said.

They all sat down and stared at one another. Dolly brought a pot of coffee and sandwiches.

"This all starts as far back as when Able raped Sheila?" Sullivan asked, as he furrowed his brow.

"Quinn, Donnell and I discussed it, and the only thing we could figure was that opportunity is the key. Able didn't know the Wrens very well, if at all. Ed Wren didn't start out to call Sheila a witch. He was distraught. Some say he promised his wife he'd bring Jenny back home alive. He couldn't bear to hold the blame when that couldn't be done, so he shifted it to Sheila." Teagan made a face. "Once she was in jail and the town was all fired up, he didn't dare tell the truth."

"Where does Gail fit in this story?" Sullivan asked.

Quinn cleared his throat. "Ed paid off the warden to tell

you Sheila was dead. But somewhere along the way, it seems he believed his own lies. Mrs. Wren never did get well. She was institutionalized and died of influenza. After that, Mr. Wren made a will that gave everything to Becca. Seems he thought Sheila was really dead and he needed to make up for his misdeeds. When he died Gail came to town to find Becca and see why the girl was to get the whole inheritance. She was upset and puzzled about the whole thing. She needed the money and the attorney who drew up the will lives right in town."

Sullivan ran his hand down his face. "When did she meet up with Able?"

"From what we heard it was from the first. She stayed at his place for a week or so and then came here asking for a job," Teagan explained.

"Stayed with him? What woman would put her reputation in jeopardy that way?" Sullivan asked.

"It's all about money," Teagan said in disgust.

"And that was when the plot was formed," Donnell said as he came inside. He took a seat and poured himself a cup of coffee. "Becca wasn't to inherit until her eighteenth birthday. Able concocted a plan where Gail married Sullivan, he'd be killed and they would take Becca. I'm not sure what they planned next, but they would have a legal right to Becca. I'm sure they would have left town for a few years."

"Or," Sullivan said as the truth dawned on him. "If she married me, she'd get Becca, the inheritance and part of the ranch. I bet she planned to double cross Able."

"But why bother with Able at all?" Quinn asked.

"If I was killed, who better to pin it on than Able?" Sullivan added.

Teagan cocked his head to the right. "Why was Able all set on getting Becca? Gail didn't come out here for nearly two years after Sheila went to prison."

"Wait. So, let me get it straight," Sullivan said, holding up one hand. "Wren promises his wife he'd bring a live Jenny back even though she was dead. Sheila is blamed for Jenny's death, and mass hysteria puts Sheila in jail. Able makes threats to take Becca, and I marry Sheila. Sheila is sent to prison thanks to Ed Wren, who paid the sheriff and the judge off. Then he paid the men at the prison to tell us Sheila was dead. Since most women don't make it out alive, he thought he wouldn't be found out. The Wrens move away and Mrs. Wren dies. So, Ed Wren had a change of heart. He writes a will giving Becca everything and then he ends up dead. Gail finds out she isn't going to inherit the Wren money, but Becca was to have it. Gail then comes here and somehow meets Able. They hatch their plan, but it all hinges on me marrying Gail. The only reason I can figure Gail needed Able was she needed someone to kill me." He glanced into the faces of everyone in the room. "What if I didn't marry Gail?"

"You'd probably have ended up with a shotgun wedding for something you didn't do," Brogan said from the doorway.

"But why did Able want Becca so badly?" Quinn asked again.

"He probably never did. I think at the time he was trying to keep Sheila quiet about who attacked her. Later it became all about the money," Teagan said, frowning. "This is getting complicated."

"You're not kidding, but things are making more sense to me," Sullivan remarked. "Now how do we get them arrested so my family will be safe?"

"I went to the next town over and sent for a Texas Ranger friend of mine," Donnell told them. "He should be here tomorrow."

Brogan grinned. "You seem to know a lot of people, Donnell."

Donnell grinned back and shrugged his left shoulder.

"We need to keep my wife and daughter safe."

"They have been. Where do you think Murphy, Fitzpatrick, Angus, Rafferty, and Shae have been? They've been swapping out guard duty with the hired men. I have to say, I'm glad nothing happened during the picnic. You are quite the gentleman."

Heat swamped Sullivan's face, and he took a deep breath. He didn't need to be in constant control of everything; he had his brothers. They had been there all along, but it was a strange revelation to him.

DONNELL'S TEXAS Ranger friend arrested Gail first, which made Able run. Two days later, he was caught too.

Sheila could finally breathe.

"You can go to the jail to see them behind bars if you like," Sullivan told her.

She shook her head. "I only want to look forward not back."

He pulled her close, and she almost felt warm. "I wish I had told you I loved you before they dragged me away to prison. It was a big regret of mine."

"I knew in my heart you loved me. I still can't believe anyone would be so cruel as to tell us you were dead." He paused and frowned. "Oh, and Becca getting Wren's money doesn't sit well with me."

She nodded. "I thought that way at first, but she suffered enough for it. It's for her future, we don't need to mention it to her now. The one thing I want most is to have your baby, but I'm still afraid."

"My sweet love, we have plenty of time by the grace of God."

EPILOGUE

*E*ven with everyone in jail, Sheila couldn't find peace. She tried and tried, but she often found herself shaking at the oddest times. They'd been to church as a family, but something wasn't right. She didn't feel God there.

A month later she went and sat in the church while it was empty. She prayed and listened to the profound silence. She'd felt God during the most awful times in her life, but now she didn't know what was going on.

She heard the door open and she turned her head. It was Sullivan. He was always near.

"I know something is wrong. Please tell me." He kneeled next to her and took her hand.

"It's hard to explain. My heart feels heavy and I should be filled with joy. I don't feel as close to God as I did. I think something is wrong with me." A lone tear trailed down her face.

"I'm certainly no expert but have you given your hurt up to God? Have you allowed him to take your worries and make room in your heart for happiness? We can't change what happened. It does no good to hate anyone involved."

She leaned over and kissed his cheek. "Go I'll be out in a few minutes."

When she heard the door closed, she closed her eyes.

Lord, what Sullivan said makes a lot of sense. Most who were involved are dead and they are Yours to forgive or not. I don't think I can give You all my hurt to take. I'm selfish and I need to remember what happened. I need to remember my journey. Please take from me all my what ifs and my blame for others. You held me through the darkness. I ask for this to be the start of a brand-new day of living in Your light. And please Bless Gemma as she carries a new life under her heart.

She felt the light and for the first time in years she felt warm. A feeling of calm bliss filled her, and she knew everything would be just fine.

LATER THAT EVENING Sheila smiled as she saw Sullivan admiring the carving she'd made on the mantel. She was pleased at the way it had turned out. In the middle were two hearts entwined with their initials inside. Next to one heart was a smaller one with Becca's initials and on the other side next to the other big heart a small heart was carved. It had the last initial K, but no first initial.

He traced his fingers over it. "This one is for someday." He turned and met her gaze.

"It's taken a lot but, in every hug, every deed, every word you have shown me how to trust you. I want to expand our family if we are so blessed. I have also learned that we can make decisions together. You have asked my opinion as though you value it, and much of my confidence has come back. I'm not all skin and bones anymore. What I'm trying to say is I love you and I'm hoping you'll meet me in the middle of the bed tonight so I can be your wife."

Sullivan took her into his arms and held her. "I take it your conversation with God went well."

"Yes, exceptionally well."

ABOUT THE AUTHOR

Sexy Cowboys and the Women Who Love Them...
Finalist in the 2012 and 2015 RONE Awards.
Top Pick, Five Star Series from the Romance Review.
Kathleen Ball writes contemporary and historical western romance with great emotion and
memorable characters. Her books are award winners and have appeared on best sellers lists including: Amazon's Best Seller's List, All Romance Ebooks, Bookstrand, Desert Breeze Publishing and Secret Cravings Publishing Best Sellers list. She is the recipient of eight Editor's Choice Awards, and The Readers' Choice Award for Ryelee's Cowboy.
Winner of the Lear diamond award Best Historical Novel-
Cinders' Bride
There's something about a cowboy

facebook.com/kathleenballwesternromance
twitter.com/kballauthor
instagram.com/author_kathleenball

OTHER BOOKS BY KATHLEEN

Lasso Spring Series
Callie's Heart
Lone Star Joy
Stetson's Storm

Dawson Ranch Series
Texas Haven
Ryelee's Cowboy

Cowboy Season Series
Summer's Desire
Autumn's Hope
Winter's Embrace
Spring's Delight

Mail Order Brides of Texas
Cinder's Bride
Keegan's Bride
Shane's Bride
Tramp's Bride
Poor Boy's Christmas

Oregon Trail Dreamin'
We've Only Just Begun
A Lifetime to Share
A Love Worth Searching For

So Many Roads to Choose

The Settlers
Greg

Juan

Scarlett

Mail Order Brides of Spring Water
Tattered Hearts

Shattered Trust

Glory's Groom

Battered Soul

Romance on the Oregon Trail
Cora's Courage

Luella's Longing

Dawn's Destiny

Terra's Trial

Candle Glow and Mistletoe

The Kabvanagh Brothers
Teagan: Cowboy Strong

Quinn: Cowboy Risk

Brogan: Cowboy Pride

Sullivan: Cowboy Protector

Donnell: Cowboy Scrutiny

Murphy: Cowboy Deceived

Fitzpatrick: Cowboy Reluctant

Angus: Cowboy Bewildered

The Greatest Gift

Love So Deep

Luke's Fate

Whispered Love

Love Before Midnight

I'm Forever Yours

Finn's Fortune

Glory's Groom

Made in the USA
Las Vegas, NV
02 July 2021